MW01015925

OVERNIGHT
SENSATION

Books by
SCOTT JOHNSON

One of the Boys
Overnight Sensation

OVERNIGHT
SENSATION

Scott Johnson

ATHENEUM 1994 NEW YORK

Maxwell Macmillan Canada
Toronto
Maxwell Macmillan International
New York   Oxford   Singapore   Sydney

Acknowledgments
Many thanks to my editor at Atheneum, Jon Lanman,
and my agent, Richard Parks, for their support all through
the writing of *Overnight Sensation*

Atheneum
Macmillan Publishing Company
866 Third Avenue
New York, NY 10022

Maxwell Macmillan Canada, Inc.
1200 Eglinton Avenue East
Suite 200
Don Mills, Ontario M3C 3N1

Macmillan Publishing Company is part of the Maxwell
Communication Group of Companies.

First edition
Printed in the United States of America
10 9 8 7 6 5 4 3 2 1
The text of this book is set in 11 point Caledonia.
Book design by Kimberly M. Adlerman

Library of Congress Cataloging-in-Publication Data
Johnson, Scott.
Overnight Sensation / by Scott Johnson. —1st ed.
p. cm.
Summary: Having acquired a new image over the summer and been accepted
by the in crowd at school, seventeen-year-old Kerry finds herself being led
into trouble and away from her real values.
ISBN 0–689–31831–6
[1. Popularity—Fiction. 2. Conduct of life—Fiction.] I. Title.
PZ7.J6367Ov   1994
[Fic]—dc20   93–23084

for Susan, my true north

I Years had been from Home
And now before the Door
I dared not enter, lest a Face
I never saw before

Stare stolid into mine
And ask my Business there—
"My Business but a Life I left
Was such remaining there?"

—Emily Dickinson

Part One

THE SAME OLD
KERRY DUNBAR

I knew for sure something was different about me when I
stepped off the bus and Billy Stockton, *Jockus Americanus,*
who in the past never even said hello unless he needed my
math homework, hauled out my luggage from the side of the
bus, looked up—and flirted.

"Can I help you with your bags?"

How would I know flirting? Believe me, even I could tell.

"No, I only live a couple of blocks from here."

"I could, uh, help you with them, to your car. . . ."

"No, really, I'll walk. But thanks, Billy."

His great smile shriveled to a mystified pucker. "I know
you, don't I?"

"Billy, it's me. Kerry Dunbar."

"Kerry . . ."

"Kerry Dunbar."

He blushed, which only made his end-of-summer tan that
much richer. He was tall, with big, wide shoulders, and good-
looking, in a kind of brawny, dim way. He shook his blond
hair out of his eyes.

"Kerry—I—you really—you really look . . ."

I looked different. I knew I did, of course, but checking
out your changes in front of a mirror with your cousin

Rhonda cooing over your shoulder was not the same as the quarterback of the football team telling you. This was proof.

Except I realized he hadn't said anything about looking *better,* just *different.* I slipped out of my daze and reached for my shoulder bag. "Anyway, Billy, thanks for asking."

"*Great,* that's what. You look great."

One little word. That's all it took to get me babbling like girls I always used to turn my nose up at. "So tell me"—could this really be my voice?—"how was your summer?"

"*Great,*" Billy blurted happily, and he launched into a week-by-week account. It wasn't so much what he said. I only half listened. It was just the notion of Billy Stockton, talking to me. I wanted to tell Rhonda. See what you've done? I would say.

"... so I worked construction," Billy rambled on, "for my dad's firm for a while. . . ."

You made football heroes talk to me on the street, Rhonda.

"I figured, I'll get a good tan. . . ."

"It's a great tan," I told him. And I meant it. That kept him going for another five minutes.

"... construction, it's almost like working out, I can bulk up for football, and when—"

It was exciting, talking to him. No, it was silly. It was—I could feel *something,* anyway, keeping me there, and it certainly wasn't my interest in how much Billy could bench-press.

"Did you say you needed a ride? I could probably—"

"I can walk, Billy. I don't live far."

It made me want to call Rhonda. Right away. To thank her for a great summer. For inviting me up, away from this town, from my mother, from—well, from *me* for a while.

I really was somebody different up there, on Uncle Artie and Aunt Karla's farm. Getting up at six and brushing down horses. Slopping in loose rubber boots through patches of cow manure. (Rhonda called them cow pies, and when they were dry you could fling them like Frisbees.) Other times, hearing Rhonda tell about college and her boyfriend Brad—it made me feel that maybe there was more to life than I had reason to expect.

And more to me. Uncle Artie said it first, just teasing. "Kerry, don't you like our cooking?" I guess I had lost nearly ten pounds by then. Another time, from Aunt Karla: "Kerry, what have you done to your hair? Your mother's not going to know you!"

What *hadn't* we done to my hair?—Rhonda and I up in her room, with the blow-dryer, her assortment of combs, and my long, straight hair that I'd been parting in the middle since I was nine. We cropped and teased it, and leafed through *Elle* and *Seventeen* searching for new challenges. Now my hair was shoulder length, cut so it revealed more of my face. Then Rhonda showed me how to give it some body. It was really the first time I had done anything special with my hair. It felt a little vain, but it was fun. So with my new hairstyle and feeling trim, and Aunt Karla saying from time to time how pretty I was, the whole summer seemed like something too big to believe.

But it wasn't just the way I looked, it was the way I felt. Grown-up and independent. Of course I knew I wasn't going to stay in high school the rest of my life, but I always supposed that the rest of life was still going to *feel* like high school. I did my best and got good grades, exceptional grades. Miss Tufts, my guidance counselor, even thought I had a chance at being selected valedictorian. But spending time with Rhonda seemed more important than any of that.

Especially the nights, when we stayed up talking. Rhonda lived in one of those huge Norman Rockwell farmhouses with about eighty-five little bedrooms tucked away, and even though I had one of my own I don't know how many nights I fell asleep on the spare bed in Rhonda's room. There was always a new adventure to listen to, something about Brad, or some wild spring break. Rhonda shared so much it made me feel it was my life, too, and I couldn't wait for what was next.

What was next happened just a little sooner than I was ready for. It started the weekend Brad came down to visit. "You'll love him, Kerry," Rhonda bubbled for a week. "We'll drive down to Ashbury, and—"

"You don't want me along," I protested. "The three of us—"

"The four of us," she grinned. And made me nag her for a day and a half until she let on who the Fourth One was. Hank, an old friend of hers from high school, who was leaving for the army in the fall. "Relax, you'll like him," she promised. Relax? Rhonda didn't understand, this wasn't just my first blind date, it was virtually my first date ever. Oh, there had been a few stiff, embarrassing outings with the type it seemed my destiny to attract: nerdy, skinny boys who started out by talking about the weather and then fell silent for the next three hours.

"And by the way," she added nonchalantly. "Hank is a real hunk."

So we made Hank the Hunk jokes the rest of the week. When I finally met him, it was no joke. I could hardly breathe. In person, he outdid my imagination. Tall and wiry in a denim jacket and snug Levi's, he kissed me hello and put his arm around me as if *we* were the old high school friends. We set off with Rhonda and Brad, who was cute enough, and sweet, but—well, no Hank. My pulse was just returning to normal a half hour into the date when he finally took off his sunglasses, and the sight of those storm gray eyes had me stammering for another ten minutes.

We sat in the front of his pickup and Hank went on in his dry, rural twang, reeling off funny comments that I picked up on a second or so late, but he didn't mind. He seemed to know exactly who I was, as if Rhonda had primed him—

Kerry hasn't been out with too many guys, Hank, go easy on her—and he wouldn't do a thing to make me ill at ease. After a bad movie in Ashbury, Rhonda wanted him to drive up to some ridge so Brad could see the sunset. He couldn't have seen too much of it, for soon all I heard from the back were the sounds of deep kisses and giggling. Hank hopped out, holding out his hand for me to follow him.

As dusk settled we walked along the overlook, leaving Brad and Rhonda alone, and just talked. We even had the same interests: he didn't want to hear about the suburbs, and I didn't want to mention them. We sat on a ledge and watched the last purple rays of light as he told me about the army, how it was a good place to learn a trade and besides, he didn't mind serving his country. At home I would have laughed, hearing that, especially around my friend Madeline; she was ten thousand percent antimilitary and usually dragged me along in her thinking. Here I was in another world, and something ached inside me to hear Hank's voice. He kissed me then, and when I pulled away, he smiled and said, "You're young," and kissed me again.

The next night he asked me out, me alone, and I said yes; I knew Rhonda would be happy to have some time with Brad. Hank drove over just about every little back road in the county, and I turned sideways in my seat, recording his gorgeous profile so I'd never forget it. He was charming in a way that didn't let on he knew the first thing about manners, or being nice, or trying to please—

Or how to seduce someone.

I guess that's what you'd call it. It was the third time we went out. Brad had gone home by then, so Rhonda had more time to pester me about Hank. I was enjoying keeping secrets, though there really weren't any secrets to tell—yet. That night there were. Hank and I were sitting in his truck, outside a Dairy Queen that was so deserted it must have sold two cones per month. The night was hot, and we were racing to eat the ice cream as it dripped down the sides of the cones.

"You got some there, around your mouth," he teased.

I reached out with my hand, already sticky, to wipe it away. He peered closer. "Nope. Still there."

I darted out my tongue. "Did I get it?"

His face was right up to mine. His eyes narrowed, intent on my mouth. "Nah," he said, "it's right . . ." Then he touched his tongue to just above my upper lip, tracing a slow curve around my mouth. I held still, even after I realized this wasn't at all about ice cream. He pulled me close and kissed me. I think I said, "Stop," but so quietly neither of us listened. This is crazy, I thought. I hardly know him, and—and then I didn't think anymore. We drove away from the Dairy Queen, but not that far. We didn't have to. You couldn't go a quarter mile before you were on some dirt road that hadn't seen a car in weeks. Hank turned off, halfway into a cornfield. With the lights off, his hands at my clothes without hesitation, the wind rustling cool through the corn husks, it was no wonder I didn't say a thing, especially not no.

The next night we went out again, and I asked him about a condom.

He laughed gently. "That's the girl's job, being careful."

"That's not what I mean." We were in his pickup again, he was holding me, and it wasn't easy getting any words out, certainly not these. "I mean, a condom for—you know, for—"

His mouth left mine for an instant. "For what?"

"For . . . well, for AIDS."

"AIDS?"

I nodded. I tried to smile, and needed one back from him.

"I'm no fag," Hank said.

"I know. But it's not—"

"Is that what all those boys in the suburbs do?"

"I don't know," I said. "I told you, I haven't, you know, done it before—"

Then I could feel him grin in the darkness. "Well, nothing wrong with that. But let me tell you, you're not going to get far asking guys to put on *condoms*." He made the word itself ridiculous. Then he kissed me. "Now, are you?"

I heard myself laugh nervously. "I guess not," I said, and tried to make a joke of it. I felt worse, for that.

Hank asked me out two nights later, and I went prepared. I brought a pack of condoms, and thought, With a little finesse we might laugh our way through it. "You should have seen me, borrowing Rhonda's car and driving three towns over and blushing like a twelve-year-old walking into that pharmacy—"

He wasn't amused. "I ain't wearing one of those," he said.

"Then"—I took a breath—"then we're not doing it."

"Well, then we're not." I never had a chance to see how strong I really was. He didn't try to pressure me, he just dropped me off at Rhonda's and drove away, not a kiss, not a word. I stood in their driveway with no place to hide, to even wipe my tears before I went inside.

I never saw him again. I talked to him once, or someone who was supposed to be him, who at least had the same voice but couldn't seem to recall he'd ever known me, not if you went by his tone, or how quickly he tried to get off the phone.

"What a jerk," Rhonda said. "I'm sorry I ever got you involved."

"All I know," I said, "is I tried to stand up for what I thought was important, and I got burned."

"Yeah, well, just hope it's the last time."

For a couple of weeks I moped. I noticed ugliness in everything about the farm: the chores were boring, the animals stunk. It wasn't as if I cared so much for Hank—I hardly knew him, I realized. And now I didn't even like what I knew. I was just angry that I'd let myself fall for that deep voice and that smooth touch, when there wasn't anything more to him than that.

I remembered standing, crying in the driveway, and I knew I never wanted to feel that way again.

By the end of the summer, though, I was better; Rhonda and her folks were special, and in my last walks around the farm in twilight I hardly brooded over Hank the Hunk at all. It was coming home that soured me now. I at least had a life at the farm—hurt though I might have been. What was there at home?

I never figured on people like Billy Stockton.

The bus had pulled away, and we stood alone in the parking lot. "I guess"—he finally passed over my bag—"I'll see you in school."

I took a step away, and so did he. "Bye, Billy," I called. He was still watching me. I motioned to my bag. "And thanks."

Thanks?

What was I *thanking* him for? What exactly *had* we talked about for five minutes? A block away I replayed the conversation in my head. Billy Stockton. Madeline would love it. Neanderthal Poster Boy, she called him. She'd want to pore over every word Billy said and together we'd hoot—

And I knew I was home. It wasn't just the heat or the bus ride or even the weight of my luggage. It was something about me that on Rhonda's farm wasn't true. I was cynical and critical and . . . defensive. Scared, even. At least up at Rhonda's I could fall for a guy, however briefly. Here, it was inconceivable. And yet, as much as Madeline and I would cut up Billy the Dumb Jock, I knew it wasn't going to convince me I hadn't really enjoyed every silly, blushing second with him. Billy Stockton, my God. Next to Hank the Hunk he seemed as comfortable as an old sweater.

I paused at the first sight of my house, as if I might spot a SOLD sign, and new people inside, and I could keep on going. But it was still mine, all right, ugly as ever, and dark, hemmed in by tall pines. If our house were a person you might have claimed, politely, that with a little fixing up she would look— all right. Inside, the ceilings were low, the rooms small. On the bookshelves were all forms of clutter, mostly knickknacks and tourist trinkets that my mother bought in secondhand shops because they were corny. She didn't get too attached to anything unless she could make fun of it in some subtle way.

I climbed the front steps and entered the hall. My mother was curled up at one end of the overstuffed sofa, reading without the light on.

"Well, I'm home," I announced.

If there was one thing that had *not* changed while I was away it was my mother. She wore her hair short, in a mannish type of cut, and favored military-looking outfits—or maybe it was just that her favorite color—khaki—made everything look that way. We hugged like amateurs. I think she was a little relieved to be able to step back and hold me at arm's length. "Let me look at you," she said.

Suddenly I was nervous: what would she notice first? My hair? That I'd lost weight? Or something more . . .

She scrutinized me, up and down, then shook her head.

"The same old Kerry Dunbar," she approved.

A stirring on the sofa gave us both a chance to look away. It was Mitzie, our raccoon-sized cat, taking time out from her nap to stretch.

"Hi, Mitzie," I said.

She snuggled down into a shape about the size of a volley-ball and dozed off immediately. I thought of the lean, preda-tory cats around Rhonda's farm. They darted through their nine lives at a pace unknown to Mitzie. She had been around forever. My parents divorced pretty early in my life, so I don't remember a lot with the two of them together. Knowing they were once married was like looking at two odd pieces of the same jigsaw puzzle—I didn't see any way they could ever have fit. I remembered a few Christmases, birthdays, and a kindergarten assembly program, but not much else. But I did remember when I was four, and we got Mitzie. I was sitting in the backseat, riding home from the animal shelter. I was struggling to hold her, she was mewing with outrage, she had already scratched me once, and from the front seat I overheard my dad.

". . . it's even worthwhile if it dies. It's good for a kid to experience death."

"Jack," my mother scolded.

"Well, it is. It's a life lesson. It gives them practice coping."

The only flaw in that thinking was that Mitzie, whom none of us ever *really* liked, apparently had no intention of dying, ever. Now, thirteen years later, long after she had outlived her role as Life Lesson for Kerry, she seemed immortal. And whenever she left a surprise on the rug, it gave my mother another chance to curse my dad.

Upstairs, in my room, my mother sat at my desk and watched me unpack. Once in a while she'd ask a question, like "How are Artie and Karla?" but they were on my father's side of the family and I knew she was just being polite. I always held back, talking to her. It wasn't that she didn't listen—she listened too well. She was a social worker, and spent long hours scanning case histories and clients' notes. Sometimes she made *me* feel like a client. Nothing I could say surprised her. She'd smile tightly, as if her teeth hurt, and nod as if anything I said were only more proof what a wry, painful world it is. I know she was hurt when my dad left her, and she never did much with her life since then except work hard at her job and get together with a few friends, also divorced. But I wanted to feel, just once, that what I said or thought *was* new. Because at least it was new to me.

I started telling her about the summer, and clipped off almost every story before I got to the end. Of course, what I could have told her, the Big Story, I didn't tell. It wasn't that she would have been shocked to learn I'd had sex with some guy (I mean, she worked with girls my age who had two or three children). No, I could tell her what I did—but I couldn't tell her what I felt. Even with Hank the Hunk growing hazier in my memory every day, that wound deep inside me was still there, it still hurt, and I wasn't going to share it with anyone unless I had a promise it would heal.

"Well, we should have something to eat," she finally said, as if dinner were some exotic custom she had just remembered. "You'll have to save the rest for later. By the way, you should call your father. He's feeling neglected, he claims."

"What's that mean?" I asked.

"That you didn't spend any time this summer with him. He needs to know you still love him, or something. So call, later. When the rates go down."

"How is Dad? Did you guys talk?"

Mom stopped by the door and seemed to think about it. "Or maybe," she said, "you could call collect this time."

After she left, I sat looking out the window. My room had the only view from the house that wasn't obstructed by other buildings or trees, and I could see the rooftops a couple of streets away. Sometimes I could see the sunset, but I had to be there at the right time. It wasn't like up at Rhonda's, where the sunset stretched itself out for an hour or so and was always waiting for you when you needed it.

2

"*Billy Stockton!*" Madeline screeched. She doubled over and clutched her stomach as if she had appendicitis.

"Cut it out," I said. "I just—"

"I'm hallucinating. That's it. Not Billy Stockton! Doctor, Doctor—"

"Madeline!"

Now she was on her knees in the middle of the sidewalk, waving her hands up to heaven. "God, take me now. I've seen it all. . . ."

By this time I was laughing, too, though I was also mad enough to seize her wrist and yank her to her feet.

"People are going to wonder about us."

"I'm *already* wondering about you," Madeline said. "*Billy Stockton.* Come *on*, Kerry. This is a big joke, right?"

"All I said was that he was really *friendly* at the—"

"I know, at the bus station, et cetera. *That's* not what I'm having hysterics over."

"What, then?"

"That the most brain-dead jock in the whole school came on to you, and you're *flattered.*"

"Just forget it."

"No, what did he say? Tell me every word."

Who was the one person I wanted to see all summer? Madeline. And who was I regretting telling a single thing to? *"Madeline."*

"Wouldn't it be priceless if he asked you out?"

"Why? You can't stand him."

"No, I mean for the laugh potential. You know what we should do? If he asks you out you say yes. Then we conceal a little tape recorder—"

"Mad, this is—"

"And at the end of the night we play it all back, what a scream! Maybe we even sell *copies*!"

Madeline had been my best friend from Before Time Began, or at least that's how it seemed. She had a knack for causing resentment in just about everybody but me. Boys especially began hating her long ago and never really stopped. If I had at least *wanted* to look more attractive to boys, Madeline went out of her way to avoid it. By sixth grade, when some girls were experimenting with makeup, Madeline abandoned dressing in any way remotely feminine. For the next two years she lived, it seemed, in the same sweatshirt and faded jeans. In high school her style changed again. For the last three years she had worn long skirts, baggy black pullover tops, and sandals. She let her thick black hair grow long, parted it in the middle, brushed it probably no more than every other day, and once in a while braided a thin strand that she coiled dreamily when deep in thought. Next to Madeline, there were times my fashion sense seemed absolutely frivolous.

Madeline was somewhere left of radical, and a lot of my ideas about politics and women's and gay rights came from her. Her parents, she said proudly, were "old New Lefties," which I didn't fully understand except that it had something to do with the sixties. There was really nothing her parents wouldn't let her do; they just wanted to "air the issues," before or after. What Madeline wanted to do was not your typical teenage rebellion: she liked to march against South Africa, boycott stores that sold irradiated foods, refuse to stand for the Pledge of Allegiance at school. She was always urging me to participate with her, and sometimes I did. Sometimes it was a lot of fun.

Once we got ourselves all worked up over frog dissection in sophomore biology. Madeline had been researching animal rights and started referring to Mrs. O'Brien, the little white-haired bio teacher, as a torturer, and how the labs were really another form of genocide, and the next thing we knew we were writing up the manifesto of the Amphibian Liberation Front, and scrawling ALF on our notebooks with drawings of frogs with little black hoods and automatic weapons. We had this big plan where we were going to sneak into the lab and let loose a bunch of frogs with ALF signs stuck to their backs. We got as far as going to the edge of the brook behind her house to gather the frogs before deciding we were too mature for something like that, and besides, the water was cold.

Now, seeing her for the first time in two months, it was supposed to be simple. I was going to walk with her to where she worked at the natural foods market, and I was going to tell a little about Rhonda and the summer. She'd say, You lost weight, didn't you? You look good. And maybe then I'd just casually refer to Hank the Hunk, just to set her up to tell her later. . . .

My mistake was mentioning Billy.

"Let's just leave him alone, all right?" I grumbled.

"You actually like him, don't you? Billy Stockton."

"I didn't say I liked him. He's just—he was just nice to me, okay?"

"You know," Madeline said with a sudden chill of seriousness, "Billy Stockton's an anti-Semite."

"He is not." The whole idea, after ten minutes of silliness, threw me. "Is he?"

"He is."

"I've never heard him say anything . . . anything about—"

"About Jews? You don't have to. You just have to look at him. Any time the subject comes up. Or *I* come around. Or, like, in December, when the teachers say, 'Merry Christmas *and* Happy Hanukkah,' and he rolls his eyes."

"But does that make him—"

"And in history last year, all the time we studied the Holocaust he was totally bored."

"Mad," I said, relieved. "He's bored with *everything*. He's a jock."

"Then why do you like him?"

"I don't," I said without thinking. "I mean, I—"

"Please," Madeline said, "don't start that I-like-him-but-I-don't-*like*-him routine."

"Okay."

We walked in silence.

"He's also a sexist, don't forget," Madeline tried after a while.

I nodded. But really, I was thinking if she was this way about Billy, how far was I from telling her about Hank the Hunk?

Then, of course, we saw Billy. He yelled my name out the window of his father's Chrysler, double-parked, and jogged over to the curb. Madeline and I were in front of the natural foods market, and when she saw him coming she fixed me with a stare and said, "I wish I had a camera. No one will believe this."

"Hey, Kerry." If Billy noticed Madeline he made a point not to greet her. She peered at him as if he were trapped on a slide in bio lab.

"What are you doing now?" he said.

"She's negotiating trade agreements with Third World nations," Madeline snapped. "What does it look like?"

I ignored that. "Well, I've got to—"

" 'Cause what you oughta do is hit the pool with us this afternoon. Perfect sun. Labor Day weekend. Last chance for the summer."

"That'd be fun. But—"

"Who's *us*?" Madeline demanded.

Billy didn't turn away from me. "Me and Todd and Greg and Heather and Heather's friend from Pierson High—"

"I can't," I heard myself sigh. "I promised I'd go read—"

"Oh, *read*," Billy groaned. "You know once school starts you're going to be forced to read for *nine solid months*—"

"What I mean is—"

"You're probably in all those AP classes, right?"

"Not really."

"I don't even know what AP *means.*"

"Or how to spell it," Madeline added.

"I'm not in AP calculus," I protested.

"Whoa." Billy reeled backward. "That means you're dumb enough for me—"

I giggled. *Giggled.* Right in front of Madeline.

She said, "*Nobody's* dumb enough for—"

"*Mad!*" I shouted. "No, Billy, I can't, I promised my mother I'd read to our neighbor."

Billy started to grimace as if I had mentioned a fatal disease.

"No, I *like to,* really. She's an elderly lady, and she's really sweet. I just read to her."

He had a look of disbelief. "Kerry, on a day like this you're going to be inside *reading* to an old—"

Madeline: "Elderly."

Billy glanced at her, irritated. "*Old* lady when you could be"—his voice rose in mock drama—"at the *pool*—"

"With sensitive types," Madeline tossed in, "like Billy."

"—where nobody's reading *anything* 'cause we're too busy having a good time. . . ."

"Billy, I'd love to—"

"Well," Madeline said, contempt oozing from her voice,

"I've got to go bag some oat bran," and in a huff she stormed into the market.

"—but I can't. I promised. And I didn't read to her all summer."

He rolled his eyes in pain.

Then asked, "Well, you need a ride?"

And I said yes.

Ms. Trice lived next door to us in an old brick bungalow. Besides reading to her I occasionally cleaned her house, mowed her lawn, did some touch-up painting. Once I even fixed a sagging gutter. She paid me for everything, even the time spent reading, though I would have done that for free.

I opened her back door—she was the only person I knew who never locked her doors—and yelled in, just in case she had her hearing aid on. Ms. Trice was unlike anyone I'd ever met. At ninety she was as sharp as a twenty-year-old. She knew a lot about politics and history, in part because, I guess, she had helped make it. Her walls were full of photographs. Mr. Trice, who died when I was nine, had taken a lot of them. But after his death, she taught herself how to use his equipment, and instead of making a shrine of the photos they already had, she added to them.

She was probably the oldest feminist in town, and her life was documented in black-and-white shots that could have come from the front pages: a band of women, one of them a young Ms. Trice, holding a banner: NATIONAL WOMAN'S PARTY. A shot of her clutching a newspaper with a headline, NINETEENTH AMENDMENT PASSED BY CONGRESS. In another, a few years later, she was standing next to Emma Goldman, whom I had read about last year in American history, smiling proudly. And there was a shot, in color this time, of Ms. Trice on a platform with younger women, all except for her dressed in the gaudy paisleys of the early seventies, holding their fists in the air. She had been *Ms.* Trice as long as I'd known her.

"I'd been waiting for that word for four or five decades," she laughed.

I found her on her sun porch. She was pretty close to deaf, and I approached her from the side so as not to startle her.

"Kerry, is that you?" She fumbled for her hearing aid—half the time she left it switched off, lying on a table—and appraised me with wonder. "Why, you look . . ."

I steeled myself. Ms. Trice didn't pull many punches.

"Like a *woman*," she said. I blushed appreciatively. In ten minutes I told her more about my summer than I had told my mother in two days. I told her *almost* everything—and I could have told her that, too. Maybe someday I would.

"Let's read; I missed your voice," she said, which meant, I knew, she missed me. She really didn't need books read aloud; her eyes were as sharp as mine. It was the voice of someone younger that she wanted. While I was growing up there was always a grab bag from the library on her table, books of history, politics, short stories, often a dozen magazines. The best part of reading to her was how much I learned. But for the last year and a half the books had been replaced by a huge pile of typed manuscript that I read slowly, in chunks. Sometimes she called it her autobiography—sometimes her memoirs—sometimes "just scribbling." It was great, whatever it was. She made every anecdote seem like a key moment (like a nine-year-old Ms. Trice attending a birth control rally with Margaret Sanger speaking); and the characters—her mother and father, her teachers, her friends and co-workers—were so lively it made the Famous Figures in my social studies text seem dull. Yet she claimed she never intended to publish it. "I'm barely halfway through," she always protested.

"Ms. Trice, you've been halfway through for almost two years, and you're still handing me new chapters."

She'd smile slyly. "It's been a busy life, Kerry."

Today's chapter was as good as any of the others. It was the story of her first boss, who called her "honey" and pinched her butt until she told him she wasn't his property; when he fired her, she tried to stage a protest rally outside his shop. . . .

But this time my thoughts diverged from Ms. Trice and her brave friends. Away from their trying to explain sexism to the cops, who only knew she was clogging up the sidewalk, and threatened her with "the paddy wagon." Away from the 1920s, or feminism, or anything that deserved a place in a book like hers.

Instead, while my lips moved smoothly over the words, I thought about Billy Stockton. How his asking me to the pool was almost . . . like a date.

"Read the part about the cop again," Ms. Trice suggested. "I'm not sure he comes across as much a bastard as he was."

I reread:

"What're you tryin' to prove, sister?" the red-faced officer demanded,

but I didn't pay attention.

I was wondering if the pool would still be open by the time I left.

3

....

"Jack Dunbar, homefinder."

Wherever he was, at the office, at home, or even in his car, my dad answered the phone that way. A real estate agent, he always claimed, "can never afford to go off duty." Once he sold a house over the phone and he never even had to get out of his pajamas. At least he said he had.

"Hi, Dad."

"Kerry? I missed you, honey. It wasn't a real Labor Day without you."

"I know. I'm sorry. It was—"

"That's okay. You can tell me all the details when you get down here."

But there was no way I could tell him everything. I couldn't believe the first few days myself. It wasn't just Billy Stockton, either. By the end of the second week I didn't even feel self-conscious when I picked my way through the crowds and headed his way, as if it were nothing to hang out with Billy and Heather Grady and Greg Del Sandro, the Megajocks and the Cheerleaders and the rest. Madeline and I had made fun of most of those people for three years now, yet all it took was one or two of them to say, "Kerry, you look . . ."

I know, different, I thought.

"So good," Heather said.

—to see they weren't anything like what Madeline and I had convinced ourselves they were.

"Tell 'em about the farm," Billy insisted.

They were just normal kids, nice, even, and before I knew it I was telling them about milking a cow, and Greg made an udder joke, and okay, it wasn't brilliant, but it was cute, and we all groaned, and I told them how I couldn't bring myself to actually squeeze the teats—"The *what*?" Billy teased—but when I finally did I sprayed milk all over. *"Gross!"* Heather yelled, "just *gross*," and we all laughed. And when the bell rang and I was already late for my first AP bio class of the year, I didn't care. My face was tingling and I couldn't have fought down my smile if I had bitten my tongue.

Could I tell Dad that?

"So you'll be coming down when?" he asked. "Late Saturday morning?"

"Well, actually, Dad, I was wondering if you would mind if I—if I didn't come down yet. Not next weekend, anyway."

"Not come down?"

"See, there's a party—I've been invited to this party—"

"A party?"

"I know, I know, I haven't seen you in almost two months—"

"A party. That's terrific. School only a few weeks old, and a party already."

"And I feel bad about not coming down—"

"Well, don't. I'll see you the next weekend, then."

"Absolutely. I promise."

"A party. That's fantastic."

Fantastic was right. I still couldn't believe it. All I knew was Billy kept referring to "the party," and finally after two or three times I was brave enough to ask, "What party?"

"At Linda Tutweiler's. You're going, right? Her parents are taking her sister back to college. Should be *devastating*."

"Well, I wasn't really invited. . . ."

"Hey, *I'm* inviting you. Okay?"

"Okay," I said, real fast, before panic or nerves or the Kerry Dunbar of the past spoke up and said no.

I brought Madeline. It was some kind of compromise between the old Kerry and the new. Bringing Madeline would let me pretend the whole evening was a joke if I had to. It wasn't easy convincing her to come. First I tried the It'll-be-fun approach, and when Madeline only stared at me as if she were worried about my mental health, I shifted to Come-on-you-owe-it-to-me-what-are-friends-for?

"*Nobody* could possibly owe *anybody* a trip to a party where *Billy Stockton* will in all likelihood be"—she shuddered—"*dancing.*"

Finally I won her with the Come-on-you'll-be-like-an-anthropologist-studying-a-primitive-culture angle. "You can even bring a notebook." That got her laughing and let me pin her down to a yes.

"I can't believe you really brought a notebook," I said, standing outside Linda's house and ringing the bell a second time. There was blaring music and squealing voices, but nobody seemed to be rushing to answer the door.

"I can't believe you wore makeup," she snapped back.

"Just a little blush," I stammered. "Anyway, put that away."

"I'm taking quotes tonight. No one will ever believe me otherwise."

I rang the bell a third time, and finally we tried the front door, which had been open all along. The music was ten times louder inside, and right next to the door a boy and a girl I didn't recognize were screaming at each other, the beer spilling out of their plastic cups—

"Quaint," Madeline muttered to me. "Can we go now?"

I pulled her inside. "Live a little." We walked down a steep flight of carpeted steps to a basement rec room, where the music was louder still, and what passed for oxygen was the mingled scent of beer and cigarette smoke. The lights were so low I only saw a crowd in the center of the room, dancing, whooping, cheering boisterously when somebody slipped and went down.

"Take a good look," Madeline said. "At graduation, when they say, 'The future is in your hands,' I want you to remember this."

We stepped over to a couch and in the darkness almost sat down before we spotted the couple already sprawled out on it, arms and legs entangled.

"Mating rituals," Madeline commented, "of the subhuman."

"Why don't you write it down," I snarled at her. I was about two seconds from suggesting we leave, but the prospect of a week of her I-told-you-so's made me hold off. Then somebody rushed over and grabbed my arm and I let out a yelp as if I were being attacked on the street.

"Kerry!" With a rush of beery breath, Billy dragged me into the herd of dancers. I tried to say something but the music was so loud we could only talk in shouted, three-word sentences.

"You look nice," he slurred between songs.

"Thanks." I was panting, and felt a film of perspiration covering me. "Billy," I said, "are you drunk?"

"I'm working on it," he grinned. He must have seen something critical in my expression, for he added quickly, "No, really, I've just had a few." Then he darted his way through the dancers, returning with a cup of beer for me.

"No, that's all right," I protested.

"Come on." He laughed. "How you gonna catch up?"

The music resumed, we started dancing, and I shrugged and sipped my beer. If I wanted a place to feel inconspicuous, there was nowhere better than in the middle of this crowd. I recognized some people I had talked to during the week, others who knew me from classes. I stumbled into Heather Grady. "Kerry!" she cried, as if we were old friends. It felt as if we were.

Billy got me another beer, and I stood off from the dancers for a song or two to catch my breath. Some of the guys were soaked through, and Kevin Montrose peeled off his shirt and threw it aside. Kevin, a huge, blubbery lineman on the football team, wasn't doing any of us any favors with his striptease.

"Kerry." Linda Tutweiler stood at my side. Linda had been in my honors classes for years, but I hardly knew her. She always seemed embarrassed by being bright, and wore extravagant hairstyles and snug-fitting skirts as if trying to make up for it. "I'm glad you could come." Her face was shining. "Did you get something to drink?"

I motioned with my cup, which now was empty, I noticed, and for some reason it sent Linda and me into hysterics. "There's plenty more," Linda said. "The keg's over by—"

"No, I probably shouldn't. . . ."

"Go *ahead.*"

I stood at the keg, waiting for the beer to reach the brim of my cup, when I heard Madeline's icy voice. "So, are you having fun?"

I should have shared something we could laugh over, Kevin Montrose's jiggling belly, or maybe the trampy outfit Donna Antonelli was wearing, but when I turned and saw how Madeline was staring at me angrily, I didn't feel like sharing anything. "I am," I said. "Are you?"

Madeline glared at my cup of beer, in the direction of the dancers, then finally back at me. "You don't even *like* beer."

"Kerry, you gotta see this." Billy swooped in and grabbed my arm. "Hey," he said after a pause, a little too drunk to notice Madeline right away. "I didn't know *you* were here."

"I wanted it that way," she said.

"I always knew you were a killer party animal." Billy laughed.

She stared at him. "Just a killer."

"Hey, you smoke?" He offered her a cigarette.

"I don't need to," she said coolly. "I've been breathing *your* smoke for a half hour."

"Too bad," Billy said, as if he didn't even notice the poison in her tone. "I wanted to show you my lighter." He laid it on his palm for her to see. It was the old-fashioned, square, re-fillable type, and on the side glass was a garish picture of a smiling girl in a bikini, her breasts thrust out, her hands behind her head. "Go on, light it," Billy said, offering it to Madeline. She backed up, as if he dangled a slug before her. "Go on."

Billy took her hand and dumped the lighter in it. "Go on. Have some fun."

Finally she rose to the dare. By now two or three others had gathered around us. On the third flick the sparks caught and held a flame, and the group started laughing.

"Wow," she looked around at them. "I guess it's true, primitive man *was* fascinated by fire."

"No, no, look," Billy pointed, leering naughtily, and we all watched the picture of the girl gradually change. At first it grew foggy, but the longer the flame endured, the more her bikini top and bottom faded from view. Soon she sat, happily naked, as if nothing mattered more than looking good to whoever had her in hand.

"Very clever." She flipped the lighter to Billy, and glanced dourly at me.

"Hey, Ker," Billy snickered, "come on upstairs." Before I could say anything to Madeline, he had dragged me halfway through the rec room, up the narrow stairs to Linda's kitchen. A bunch of people stood around the table, surrounding a girl in a chair. When she dipped her head back, I saw the glass in her hand and part of the drink sloshing down her face and hair, and the group let out a massive cheer.

"Who's next?" somebody yelled, and somebody else demanded, "A quarter, come on, a quarter." Billy dug in his jeans and slapped one onto the table.

"What's going on?" I tried to whisper to him.

He shouted, "Playing quarters." Then, an idea. "Hey, you guys, let Kerry play. Come on."

"No, that's all right," I protested, but things happened fast after that. Billy and another boy led me to the chair, and the girl reluctantly gave up her spot. They sat me down and I felt I had stumbled into some mad dentist's office. Someone pulled my hair back, someone else dropped Billy's quarter into a glass, and another poured in some clear liquor.

"But wait, I—"

"Come on." Billy massaged my shoulders. "One big gulp. Win the quarter. Down the hatch."

"Down the hatch!" they all chanted. "Down the hatch!"

"Kerry Dunbar playing quarters," I heard another voice. "Somebody take a photo."

The chant started up again, and I grabbed the glass and tried to gulp it down.

I needed three swallows, with some of the drink dribbling down my chin. For a moment I wondered if I would ever breathe again, the liquor burned so hot inside me, but at the end I fished out the slimy quarter and held it up, to everyone's delight. They cheered. Billy hugged me.

I won one more quarter and told Billy I had to go down to find Madeline, but she was gone by then, of course. I was angry that she had left, and then I felt guilty, and then I was angry that I felt guilty. I talked for a while to Heather and Linda. I don't remember a word that we said, except that talking to them seemed the easiest thing in the world. They laughed and they listened and they didn't make me think I had to *analyze* what I said in *advance,* as I sometimes did for

Madeline. Then we were all dancing again, and I stopped feeling bad about Madeline. In fact, I forgot about her. Some of the guys on the football team decided to scrimmage in the middle of the dance floor, lining up and running disorganized plays while the music blasted. People laughed and applauded and *oohed* when two guys butted heads and went down.

By then I had had more than enough to drink, and I wasn't feeling so great. The rec room was a mob of confusion. I climbed the stairs with difficulty. Fresh air was what I wanted, and it was time to walk home—slowly.

Outside Linda's front door Billy was waiting.

"You're leaving, too?" I said. All of a sudden I felt very naive.

"What the hell," he shrugged. "Keg's empty."

Then we were in his dad's Chrysler. I rolled down the window. "So," Billy slurred. I noticed his driving wasn't a lot better than his pronunciation. We took corners in wide arcs and only paused a half second at stop signs. "You coming to the game next week?"

I said sure, I guess so, and he asked me again, as if he hadn't heard me, and then he fell silent for a couple of blocks. He drove intently now, staring straight ahead, slumping a little in his seat and pulling himself up again. There was an eerie feeling in the car—as if I were at the beach and the rest of the swimmers had returned to shore and I was out there rolling happily among the waves while a shark was circling quietly, stealthily. . . .

Billy pulled over along a dark street, in the shadows midway between two streetlights, and flung away his cigarette.

"No," I said, "I live a couple of blocks up ahead—"

"That's okay." He pulled me to him. "We'll get there, don't worry."

"But I—"

He kissed me hard, sort of mashing my nose while he did it. I wasn't sure I wanted to be kissing Billy Stockton, and while he kissed me again I thought, Lighten up, you're *already* kissing Billy Stockton, what's the big deal? While I was carrying on this little debate Billy put his hand on my breast and I must have jumped a foot.

"You ticklish?" he murmured.

"Not exactly." It was hard to talk with his lips all over mine (I guess that was the point), and now it all seemed like work: I had to use my right hand to keep track of his left, which was roving all over. In that instant I had a memory of cornfields and the deceptively tender grip of Hank the Hunk. It made me shiver, and I started to lean back, away from Billy's kisses, in panic. He took it the wrong way.

"If we go in back," he whispered, "there's more room."

"In back?" It was strange, but part of me felt like laughing. I knew then, jittery as I was, that this was nothing like what happened in the summer. With Hank the Hunk I was drowning, and I clung to him for safety all the while he pulled me under. But that was secret now, far away, and final. Here, in Billy's car, on a block not too far from my own, I was in control. I still had to push him off—but I knew I could say no to him in a way I never could with Hank. . . .

I fiddled behind me, releasing his hand for a moment while I groped for the door handle. That gave him a chance to paw me all the more until the door swung open suddenly and both of us spilled out in a heap. I slid out from beneath him. "I've got to go, Billy." He had a tough time even sitting up, and he looked dazed. I was already halfway down the street, tossing back an embarrassed good-bye, when he started to throw up. I tried to keep going, but I couldn't. He looked so pitiful there, in the darkness, still half sprawled across the front seat and vomiting into the curb.

Hesitantly, I approached. "You okay?" I called.

He said something like "Urghh," lifted himself up onto all fours, and shook his head.

"Billy?"

"Damn," he croaked.

"Are you . . ." I stepped closer. "How about if I drive you home?"

"Argkk. *Ack*." He turned to spit several times. "Eh-hmm." I took that as okay.

I was still wary as I got behind the wheel, but he wasn't about to go pouncing on anybody for a while. I probably shouldn't have been driving myself, but I took all the turns carefully and waited at the stop signs the way you never do except in driver's ed, and I'm not sure how long it took, but we made it to Billy's house. I'll get home okay, I thought. I want to walk. It'll clear my head. I don't mind. That's what I would say, just in case he asked.

I helped him out of the car, pointed him up the driveway to the door, placed the keys in his palm, and kissed him lightly on the cheek.

He never asked.

4

From way up on the top row of the stands where I sat, it was almost impossible to keep track of Billy. Once the ball was snapped, I lost him among the frantic zigzags of helmets and blue jerseys. From time to time I cheered, like the other fans—"Let's go, Wildcats!"—but my wavering, weak tone sounded funny. Beside me Madeline concentrated on a novel. We sat up there, at the very top, at her insistence. Every drumroll or cymbal crash annoyed her. The first few times I cheered she only glanced up with a condescending smirk. Now I could tell she was getting restless. The wind whipped her hair around, and she sighed angrily after every play.

"It's bad enough," she said, slamming the book shut, "you drag me to that spectacle at Linda Tutweiler's a couple of weeks ago, but now you insist on making me a—a *sports fan.*"

"Just relax." I wasn't ready to admit that I wasn't fascinated by it, either. "Enjoy the game."

She raised her voice to assault level. "You should be happy, though. Those are all your friends down there."

"Mad, please . . ."

"Well, they are. You talk to them in the halls. You go to their *parties. . . .*"

"What have I done that's so wrong?" I turned to her. "I made some new friends. Excuse me."

"And you abandon your old friends. Did you ever wonder what happened to me that night?"

"You left. I figured that out."

"And you still won't tell me what happened after I left."

"Nothing happened," I said. "And if you're so curious, why didn't you come to that party last week at Eddie Fallender's?"

"I'm sure they're all the same."

Not really. I'd become *much* more assured at quarters. "Let's just watch the game, okay?"

She stood up, shoving her book into her knapsack. "I'd rather conjugate French verbs." She stepped down to the next row, and suddenly looked back. "You're really not different, you know."

"What's *that* got to do with anything?"

"These people might think you are because, I don't know, your *hair*, and because you *dance* with them, but you're not different. You're still Kerry. And they'll probably be disappointed when they realize that."

"Thanks a lot."

She shrugged, and stepped down another row. "Stop by the store tomorrow." She picked her way carefully down the tiers of seats. It was about the most athletic feat I had ever seen her perform.

I thought about what she said. It didn't leave me any less angry that she was right, of course. How can a person change in just a couple of months? But life sure *seemed* different. Where Madeline was wrong was thinking the real Kerry never wanted to have some fun, to feel more popular. I liked the feeling.

And now, self-conscious at being so conspicuous, all alone at the top of the stands, I began to make my way toward the groups of people below. Over the loudspeaker I heard Billy's name announced. He must have done something good, his teammates were patting him on the butt and high-fiving him. "Let's go, Billy!" I shrieked, in my reedy new sports-fan voice, and then I heard my own name called out.

I glanced around, and saw only kids and parents peering out at the field.

"Kerry Dunbar. Hey. Get over here."

A tall, lean, dark-haired boy motioned me to him insistently. Kyle West. He was a basketball player, a subtle threat to most teachers' authority, and, I had to admit as I bumped past people's shins, one of the best-looking guys in the senior class. "Hi," I said softly.

"Come on, sit, *sit.*" He patted the bench beside him. "This is the big touchdown drive. You don't want to miss it."

I sat hurriedly, and for the next five minutes we didn't once look down at the field.

"Since when do you have school spirit?" he teased. "I always thought you were too *intellectual* for this stuff."

No, not at all, I tried to tell him. I just never followed sports that closely. It was good to get involved. Recreation is so important. I wasn't quite sure just what I was chattering, for all the time I was really studying his face. Whatever angle you were looking at *had* to be his best—until he shifted a notch and he looked even better. He leaned back, muscular but slim, crossing his long legs, sizing me up without hesitation. He had the delicate fingers of a piano player, and it was sad to imagine them wasted on a basketball.

"So the point is, you're not a stiff after all."

"A *stiff*?"

"Well"—he grinned to relax me—"that's how you always seemed to me. Before."

"I—"

"I could be wrong."

"I think you were wrong." I grinned right back at him. I knew I was being teased, and I liked it. Kyle was one of those presences in the classroom that you knew teachers hated but kids enjoyed. He never got in trouble himself, but he had an uncanny ability to mutter something when the teacher wasn't looking, and always draw a ripple of snickers.

"Well, you definitely weren't a stiff at Eddie Fallender's."

"You were there?"

He cocked an eyebrow. "I was watching you."

How did I miss that? I wondered. Just then the crowd let loose with a roar and I saw several of our players hugging each other in the end zone. Around us everyone was standing, so Kyle and I climbed to our feet and cheered with them. The band started playing. Somebody threw confetti. The cheerleaders were kicking out on the field.

We never once mentioned the score.

"You know how to party, that's for sure," Kyle said.

"I'm really just learning," I told him. "Anyway"—I motioned toward the field—"I guess we're winning."

"Looks like it," Kyle said, though he kept his eyes on me. "So you're going out with Billy Stockton."

"Oh, not really. Well—," I stammered. "Just to parties . . . I mean . . . it's nothing. . . ."

"He's a good athlete," Kyle said, rescuing me.

"He really is," I agreed.

"Too bad about the arm." For the first time he drew away from me and stared thoughtfully down at the field.

"What about his arm?"

"Well, it's fine, I suppose, for high school ball. But they're looking for *velocity* and *accuracy*. That's—"

"Who's *they*?"

He turned back to me, surprised.

"The colleges."

"Oh."

"I mean, he could probably *play*, for some little school somewhere."

"We haven't really talked about college." We hadn't really talked about anything, I wanted to say.

"But it'd be tough for him to nail down a scholarship."

Kyle's attitude was starting to gall me. "You seem to know a lot about it."

"I've been studying the options. For scholarships." I must have looked confused. "You know. For basketball. I play *basketball.*"

"Oh, duh. Of course. I was thinking—"

"You know," he went on, smiling, "the game with the iron hoop, the orange ball—"

"Okay, *okay,*" I said, and laughed.

"If I were Billy, I wouldn't be tossing those long bombs."

I didn't care enough about football to ask him to explain. I only said, "We seem to be winning."

"I'm not talking about *winning.* I'm talking about scholarships. If I were Billy I'd be presenting myself more carefully. His problem is, he *exposes* his weaknesses."

"But don't you just play your best and hope some school makes you an offer?"

Kyle snorted. "Sure. If you just want to *hope.* But if you want to steer yourself to the best possible school—"

"You wouldn't throw long passes."

"You wouldn't do *anything,*" he corrected me patiently, "that would keep you from looking good."

Around us the fans were counting down the last few seconds of the game. A muffled gunshot sounded, everybody rose and cheered, and more confetti drifted by.

"You've got it all figured out." I was a little annoyed—and a little intrigued.

"Well," he said, as we followed the crowd down to the field, "just enough."

"Is that how you play?" I asked. "So you look your best?"

"Why don't you come see this season?"

"I might." I smiled.

"Now that you're such a sports fan."

Then a couple of parents got between us, and before I

knew it I was at field level, and Kyle was gone. The players and cheerleaders were leaning over the frail chicken-wire fence that separated them from the stands. I saw Billy's number twelve, and his face brightened when he spotted me. "Hey, Ker," he called out, and yanked his helmet off.

I ran up to the wire, leaned across, and kissed him. "You were great," I said.

"Aww." He looked a little surprised. "I was okay. . . ."

"No," I insisted, and I kissed him again. "You were great." I pulled a step back and scanned the crowd nonchalantly. Billy had his arm around me by then. I arched to the side a little to keep his muddy uniform off my jacket.

"Kerry," I heard. I turned eagerly toward the voice. It couldn't have been anyone more disappointing. Mr. Hyams, the economics teacher, stood on the first row of the bleachers, smiling blandly and holding up his right hand in the peace sign.

"Oh, God," Billy groaned. "Mr. Relevant. I'll see you later." He kissed my cheek and trotted with the rest of the team toward the locker room.

Mr. Hyams hopped down and hurried over to me. I could never look at him directly. His blue eyes were as empty as a blank TV screen. The kids called him Mr. Relevant because it was his favorite word. "The unemployment rate. That's *relevant*," he'd say. He flashed the peace sign constantly. You could tell it embarrassed most of the teachers and they tried to ignore him when he did it, but some of the kids flashed the peace sign back to him, dropping their index fingers when he wasn't looking and twisting their wrists around. He never noticed. Mr. Hyams got his politics from the sixties, his clothes from the seventies, and his bald spot from the eighties. And it was just my luck, he liked me.

"Kerry Dunbar," he greeted me. "Our president."

"President?" I asked.

"Of the Green Earth Club."

"Oh. Right." It was the school environmental group. I had helped to form it two years ago. And I had completely forgotten I was elected president last spring.

"You're all set for our meeting Wednesday at lunch?"

"Of course," I lied, and Mr. Hyams blathered on: how there were all sorts of new issues to address, and freshmen to get involved, and projects, and I nodded at every word, only wishing he would go away. And once I glanced up and there was Kyle West, several rows back in the stands, his arms crossed casually, smiling down at me. *Enjoying* my discomfort.

"It'll be a great year, Ms. President," Mr. Hyams promised, "if you're totally committed."

"I am," I said. "Totally."

5

....

"Are you wearing makeup?"

We were on our way to AP European history when Madeline stopped under one of the hall lights and peered so closely at me I thought she was counting my pores.

"Just a little mascara," I mumbled.

"To school," she said, almost to herself. "Now she's wearing makeup to school."

This time she wasn't going to get me feeling guilty. "So what if I am?"

"You know a rabbit probably went blind just so you could *think* you look better."

So much for not feeling guilty.

She continued: "At *least* one rabbit. Probably dozens, by the time they perfected those *chemicals* you have on your lashes."

"Come on, Mad. It's just mascara. Hardly anyone notices it."

"Kerry, don't you have any principles left?"

"I can't believe you're making such a big thing out of—"

"Out of torturing animals? What's next, a fur coat? Let's club some baby seals?"

"You know why you're saying this? Because of the scholarship, that's why." The first weekend in November Madeline and her parents were flying to Michigan. She was a finalist in the National Science Fair Scholarship Competition, and our entire school's science department thought her project on "nonabusive cosmetics testing" had a good chance to win. "You're just nervous." I knew that wasn't true, she'd be railing at me about makeup whenever I wore it, but I jumped for any kind of edge to use against her.

"Nervous? All the scholarship money in the world isn't worth one poor blind rabbit—"

"All right," I raised my voice. "*All right*. I'll go in and take it off." I turned toward the girls' bathroom.

So crucify me, I thought, going through the doorway. I wore a little makeup. There was already someone at the sink, so I dawdled behind her, pretending I had nothing better to do.

"Hi, Kerry."

I looked in the mirror and saw Linda smiling back at me.

"Hi," I said lukewarmly.

"What's wrong?" She dabbed at her nose and her cheeks with a wadded up paper towel.

"Nothing. I'm fine."

"Did you want to use the mirror?"

"Oh, no," I protested, then realized what else would I be standing there for? "I mean, yes. No hurry, though."

"How's it going with Billy?" She backed off from the sink, gauging her reflection from different angles.

I muttered something like, "Couldn't be better," then fumbled in my purse for some tissues. Linda hovered behind me. I knew she just wanted to chat, but it made me nervous. When the bell rang, I dropped the tissues in the sink.

Then she said, "You have such pretty eyes."

I looked up at her reflection over mine. "I do?"

"They're really nice. Especially with that color." She gestured to the pale yellow top I had bought with Rhonda that summer.

"You know what you need?" Linda said. "Just a touch more."

I felt a little dazed. "More?"

"More mascara." She came up to me at the mirror. "Right . . . here." She pointed.

I glanced quickly at the reflection. "Well, actually," I began, "I was going to—"

"Want me to help you?"

I thought of my class, and of Madeline, and then I thought of how nice it was to be told that something about me was pretty, and not feel *guilty* for it.

"Sure," I said.

"Hold still." She took the brush. "Look up."

"Aren't you supposed to be in history, too?" I asked her.

"Um-hmm." Linda concentrated on my lashes. "I guess feudalism is going to have to wait."

I started to giggle, and so did she. "Hold still," she scolded, and we giggled all the more.

I didn't wear any makeup for the first Green Earth Club meeting. It wouldn't have fit. Good thing, too. Mr. Hyams couldn't just let me sit at a desk and get the meeting started from there. He insisted I go up to his podium, where, I imagined, the group had a real chance to check me out. They probably didn't. They weren't the kind to care who did what to her hair, or wore what clothes, or went to whose parties. But these days I felt everybody's eyes on me.

"Robert's Rules of Order," Mr. Hyams reminded me as kids trudged into the room. "Motions, seconds, votes."

"Hi," I said to half a roomful of students. "Uh, welcome." And while I struggled to say more, because truthfully I hadn't given a second's thought to the Green Earth Club in about four months, I looked out at them. What a collection: Madeline in the front row, with notes and newspapers. Next to her Andrew Claridge, the closest thing to a friend Madeline had among the male gender, a small, polite science fanatic ("the best lab partner ever," Madeline claimed). Jessica Oliveri, a really sweet, pretty sophomore girl with long auburn hair who, for some reason, idolized me. And in a chair by the window, concentrating on peeling an orange while keeping the rind all in one section as if he were performing surgery, was Teddy Mattson, a . . . well, I didn't know how to describe Teddy Mattson. He was tall, and kind of cute the way a scruffy old teddy bear is. He had long thin blond hair, an earring, he wore tie-dyed shirts under button-down Oxfords, and impossibly large sweaters that billowed on him like ships' sails. He went sockless in winter and wore hiking boots and wool pants on the hottest days in spring. He certainly wasn't a jock. He wasn't a brain (though he was in my AP English class). He wasn't a metalhead, he wasn't a neohippie. He could return the peace sign to Mr. Hyams so it was sincere and a spoof at the same time. Most people just thought he was crazy. I guess I did, too.

I stared out at these people and the others, and I felt depressed.

"Are we having a meeting or not?" Madeline prodded.

"Okay," I said. "Welcome to the first meeting of the Green Earth Club."

Mr. Hyams started cheering and clapping his hands. "Let's make a difference!" he called out. It sounded pretty weak.

"Okay," I tried again. "So does anyone have any ideas on . . . on any projects. . . ?"

I was already a disaster up there. All I wanted was my lunch, and to be somewhere else. Last year, when the twenty-odd members voted me president, it felt like a triumph. I was really proud, though hardly anybody in the whole school had even heard of the Green Earth Club. In the two years the club had existed we had accomplished a few things. Mostly we organized cleanup outings, and once we met for fifteen minutes with our state senator. Last year the state adopted a bottle bill, which required a nickel deposit on soda and beer bottles, and because we had written letters to the newspapers and collected signatures, we felt a part of that new law—we felt special.

Now, looking around the room, I saw us as a band of outcasts, oddballs, and nerds, with a nerdy teacher adviser—and, I reminded myself, look who they chose as president.

I hemmed and hawed, asking for old business and new business just as Mr. Hyams wanted me to, and the group was getting restless until Andrew suggested we do something about recyclable trash, and everybody got excited.

"We can return those soda and beer cans, you know," Andrew said, "and build up our treasury. There's money just *lying* there on the side of the roads."

"That's right" and "Why not?" and "My dad's got a pickup we could use," voices bubbled.

Madeline turned to the rest. "Why don't we get together the Saturday after next and collect as much as we can that's recyclable? We could get aluminum cans, and glass—"

"Some places take old tires."

"How about tin cans?"

"We wear gloves, and bring big garbage bags—"

"The second Saturday from now, at ten o'clock, how's that?"

Mr. Hyams chided me. "President Dunbar?"

"Okay, listen." I raised my voice, and just as everybody fell silent I said without thinking, "Wait, there's a *game* that Saturday."

Fourteen blank, stunned faces gazed up at me.

Finally someone in back asked, "What game?"

A boy who wore a strap to keep his glasses on said, "A football game, I'll bet. Isn't this football season?"

Someone else: "God, who cares?"

Madeline, softly and snidely: "Friends of the quarterback care."

"I just thought," I stammered, "some of us might be planning to go to . . . to the game. . . ."

Suddenly Teddy Mattson called over from the windows. "Let's *all* go to the game. Let's storm the stands at halftime. Let's *shame* people into recycling. If we catch somebody throwing away a can, we all surround him and chant *polluter* or *ecocriminal* or—"

"Thank you, Teddy, thank you," Mr. Hyams said. He stood. "I think we'll get a lot of recyclables if we go out to the lake. The hills behind the beach are full of refuse. I'll get the minivan from the school. What we need now—"

"Wait. Don't tell me. Committees," Madeline groaned.

"That's right," he said. "One committee to organize the day, and another committee for publicity—"

"Wait, wait, Mr. Hyams!"

"Yes, Teddy."

He cradled the orange peel in his hands. "Why don't we have a float in the homecoming parade?"

As if on cue, we all said, "A *float*?" We sounded like a kindergarten class.

"We decorate an old truck with cans and bottles and tires and cardboard and newspapers—we make it the ugliest thing around, and we have slogans like Save the Earth and Recycle—"

I wondered if Teddy should be on medication.

"—and then at the end of the parade we rip it all apart to show how all of that stuff can be *reused,* so we not only get *publicity,* we *educate* people—"

I looked for Mr. Hyams to shut him up, but he had a curious smile, and he stroked his chin while Teddy's idea flickered around the room like one lost match igniting a forest.

"I like it," Madeline said. "Why should homecoming just be for the jocks?"

Everybody liked it. Mr. Hyams had us all break up into committees, and Teddy's Homecoming Committee was the wildest, noisiest of them all. At first I stood at the podium, picking at my sandwich, and then I drifted unnoticed from one committee to another, standing by as if listening before I felt self-conscious and moved on to the next.

"That's the way, President," Mr. Hyams said to me. "You delegate the responsibility, and you monitor the results. You're learning."

I nodded. He pulled a desk up to one of the groups. I stayed up front.

What I was learning was how left out of all of this I felt.

I watched Billy from the passenger seat as he drove with his fingertips on the wheel, the can of beer nestled between his legs. "Crash and Trash!" he whooped, and Kevin Montrose yelled the same, "Crash and Trash!" Linda and Heather and Greg, all crammed in the backseat, sang along. It was supposed to be cool, Crash and Trash, like the way heavy-metal bands destroyed their hotel rooms after a concert. Just find a place, a backyard, a summer cottage with a cheap lock, even a toolshed if it was big enough. Slip in through a door or a window, make yourself at home, down a six-pack or two, leave when you were done. Let the maid clean up the mess. Linda and Heather and I had fun goofing on how seriously the guys seemed to take it. I guess it let us all feel kind of daring without really causing any harm.

I was surprised that I'd had so much to drink already. It seemed most of the time I was trying to talk people out of getting drunk, or out of trying to get *me* drunk. But lately I knew I'd been drinking more. It was easier and easier to do. There was a way friends could hand you one drink after another so you lost track of how many you'd had until the number came clear about the same time the room started spinning. I wasn't at that state yet, but I wasn't too thrilled about Billy driving if he felt at all as I did.

"We should go out by the lake, nobody's in those cottages now," Greg called from the back. "We could find some place."

"Too far," was all I could manage to say.

"We need a place *bad!*" Billy roared, laughing.

Linda stuck her head between the front seats. "Kerry, what about Madeline Abraham's house? What's that like?"

"Madeline's?" I sputtered. "But—why—"

"She's gone, isn't she? Isn't she in Michigan?"

"I don't—I don't know—"

"Michigan?" Billy turned to us. "That's perfect!"

"Didn't they wish her good luck over the loudspeaker in homeroom yesterday?" Linda tried to remember. "Some kind of contest or something . . ."

"Well let's *go,*" Heather whined, "and get out of this *car.*"

"What about it, Ker?" Billy asked.

It was all too ridiculous to even consider, Crash-and-Trashing Madeline's. *Impossible,* I wanted to say—

Kevin's voice, thick and drunk: "We're going to *Michigan?*"

I heard my laughter, high and giddy above the others—

"No, moron." Billy grinned at Kevin, then turned to me. "What the hell did she go to Michigan for?"

I took a deep breath to try to answer. Suddenly it seemed the funniest reason in the world, and the word exploded like a sneeze. *"Bunnies!"*

The car rocked with laughter. Another beer can popped open and the sound of that was funnier still.

"Safe. Testing." My tongue was a size too large for my mouth. I kept trying. "Different ways to . . . so it . . ." I finally swallowed and yelped, "So it won't hurt the bunny." By now I felt a little guilty. "It's not funny," I protested, but I had to bite the insides of my mouth to stop giggling. I forced out the words like a toddler learning to speak: "Non-a-bu-siv . . . testing."

"That's the dumbest thing I ever heard," Kevin said. That set everyone off again.

Billy glanced over. "So where's she live?" And the next

thing I knew, we had parked one street over and were drifting in ones and twos down the sidewalk toward her house.

"I don't think this is"—all I heard were my exaggerated *s*'s as I slurred—"such a good idea."

Billy propped me up with one strong arm. At the corner of the Abrahams' lot I heard whispers, and one voice, Greg's, delighted. "They got a garage. Perfect!"

Even as we all slipped through the front gate, running in a crouch like commandos on a raid, I heard myself tell them, "I don't think we should do this." But who was listening? I brought up the rear.

The garage was detached from the house. While the rest of us clustered for cover under a tree, Billy first tried the side door. Then, flattening himself along the wall, he came to a little window. He banged with the heels of his palms until it gave way, and he inched it up. He pushed aside some curtains, and wriggled in as if the garage were swallowing him. A second later the side door opened with a squeak you could have heard in Michigan.

Somebody helped me inside.

Two or three beer cans popped open before anyone even whispered. Then a nervous laugh or two. I heard the *clink* of Billy's lighter, and the interior was illuminated dimly. The car was gone, probably left at the airport, so there was a big space in the center, and clutter everywhere else: old bicycles, a workbench, shelving, lawn chairs against one wall.

"What a dump," Kevin said.

"It's just a garage," I tried to snap back. "What'd you expect?" I had been there dozens of times, helping Mad with projects and chores through the years. That didn't make it feel any less like trespassing.

Everybody fashioned a place to sit. Billy led me to a corner.

"What's with the newspapers?" Greg wondered. Nearby I could make out eight or ten stacks of them, bundled neatly.

"For recycling," I said, before Billy pulled me onto his lap and kissed me. I squirmed free. "She wants to set up a program for—"

"Tell him later." I could feel him grin in the darkness as he kissed me again.

For a while, except for no music or bellowing voices, it might have been just another party. Greg and Heather were giggling quietly across the way, Kevin was stumbling around in the dark, and I tried to limit Billy's passion to a level I could manage.

To show how out of my head I really was, I first thought the sound was a snake. *Ssssst.* A huge invisible snake, just like in a fairy tale, preying on the silly fools who dared to venture into the mysterious castle—

Was I already in a dream, or just drunk?

No, there, again. *Ssssst.*

"What's that?" Linda snickered.

Sssssst. Sssssst.

Greg found a flashlight on the workbench. The spotlight flickered around the room and made me dizzy. I pushed Billy back and gulped some air.

"Look who's here," Heather laughed. "Picasso."

With a can of spray paint he must have found on a shelf Kevin was doodling graffiti on one bare wall. You could see him grinning as he swayed gently, but he didn't respond to our taunts. In time the aimless squiggles turned into a recognizable shape . . .

"It's a gingerbread man," Heather hooted. "It figures. He's hungry."

Then, on the chest, he drew two huge breasts with nipples.

"You pig, Kevin," Linda said.

Below the figure he wrote "Madaline."

Greg laughed, then Billy, too. It gave me a chance to ease away from him. "Kevin," I called. "Stop it." I sounded like one of those mothers in a supermarket whose kid is racing away with the cart.

"Kevin," Billy said. "You ought to write that joke we saw in the john."

Kevin nodded, and moved to a blank spot closer to us.

"What joke?" I asked, wary.

"This is great, listen," Billy said. "It's in the second-floor john. 'Who are the three ugliest girls in the school?'"

A few seconds of suspense, just Kevin chuckling to himself. "Tell 'em," he mumbled.

Billy blared, "Number one, Madeline Abraham, number two, Madeline Abraham, number three, Madeline Abraham."

"Kevin, stop!" I cried. The snake kept hissing as the letters formed. "You're going to write that?"

"Nope," Kevin answered, and laughed.

What he wrote was far worse. I couldn't make out everything. I didn't need to. I only needed to see *Jew bitch* and a lopsided Star of David to make me think how content I would have been with bad jokes from the bathroom wall.

"Kevin!" I shouted. I got ssshed by Linda and Greg, and I turned to them. "Look what he's doing." I ran up to him and grabbed for his arm. "Stop it." But he was way bigger than I and with nothing more than a naughty grin he brushed me aside and kept on.

"Billy." I ran to where he lounged against some newspapers. "Make him stop."

"Ker, relax, they can paint over—"

I pushed him up so he could see. "Look."

Billy wavered a bit, then stood tall. "Oh, Jeez." He shook his head.

"See?" I said.

"Hey, Kev," he called. Well, about time you speak up, I thought, and looked around for something to blot out the lettering.

But Billy only asked, "You got a smoke?"

I watched Kevin dig out a cigarette and fling it at Billy. And as if unable to look away, I watched Kevin's letters form words—words I had always known existed, words I had seen on a wall once from a passing train, scribbles in the back of a school copy of Anne Frank's *Diary of a Young Girl,* slurs occasionally scratched on a desktop or tattooed on some neo-Nazi's arm on "Oprah."

Billy nestled back onto the stack of papers and reached out to me.

Words I never really believed could be.

"Billy," I pleaded.

"Kevin," he sneered. "You idiot." He turned to the rest of us. "Look how he spells *synagogue*."

I heard a laugh or two. Even Kevin chuckled, his head nodding in a drunken trance. Then he turned with the can and faked a squirt at Billy. "Who you calling idiot?"

Billy didn't flinch. "Dipshit." He laughed, then flipped back the top of his lighter and thumbed the flint.

Exactly as Kevin aimed the can again, and this time, sprayed him.

The spark of the lighter ignited the stream of paint and flared up with a sudden whoosh. For a second the garage was bright with a rush of white-orange light. Billy yelped in fright and kicked his legs to back away, falling to the floor. He flung the lighter, still burning like a torch, toward the open side door. There was a sickly smell and a faint hiss that I could still hear after the lighter clattered on the concrete and the flame went out.

Billy cursed, rubbing at his face. Kevin cackled high and crazy. Billy lunged for him. I caught his arm, and Greg, laughing as fiercely as Kevin, tried to help me hold him back.

Then the hiss turned louder, and I heard a rush of air like a thousand flags snapping in the wind. Near the side window I watched the fringed bottoms of the curtains consume themselves in flames.

I turned to hunt for a fire extinguisher. There must have been shouting, but all I could hear was my heartbeat, pounding the way it does when you're deep underwater and your breath is running out. Then I heard Heather's voice. She was giggling. I froze, self-conscious at my panic, and looked back. Maybe it wasn't so bad. One of the guys had knocked the flimsy rod from the window, and now Billy and Kevin and Greg were taking turns stomping at the flames as the burning curtains lay against the base of the wall, laughing at one another as they did. Greg leaped back with a squeal of pain, hopping on one foot, grinning foolishly.

Kevin reached over and tried to douse the fire with a beer. "You oughta piss on it," Billy said. "You had a six-pack."

While they jeered at each other I saw their faces suddenly highlighted in a burst of brighter orange. They drew back, and one insistent lick of flame shot up to the window, followed by another, and then several, as if to seize the window ledge and pull itself up. The wallboard around the window puckered and turned a charcoal black. Soon the whole window was framed in fire.

In the flickering glow I saw how white Linda looked, and I knew how scared I was. "Get something to smother it!" I yelled, and I peered over Billy's shoulder, up into his face, where his smile had faded into utter confusion.

Smoke spiraled from stacks of newspapers to our left. My eyes itched furiously.

"Shit," Kevin said numbly.

"It was those goddamn rags, where the curtains fell." Greg's voice was higher than I'd ever heard it. "Why the hell did they leave those goddamn rags lying around—"

"Help me find something"—my voice cracked in a deep cough from the smoke—"to stamp it out—"

"And those newspapers," Greg continued hysterically, "if they didn't have those news—"

"Shut the hell up!" Billy yelled at him. "We gotta get out of here."

"Help me!" I seized his arm. The garage was full of smoke, and flames crawled up from the bottoms of

more newspapers as the edges of the stacks curled blackly.

"Forget it," Billy said, and took my hand.

"No!" I shouted, as if the fire were really just a question of willpower, it could all be corrected, but if we let down for even an instant—

He yanked me to the door. He had one arm around me in a kind of headlock, but with each step I fought loose and looked back, as if the next time I'd be rewarded and see the fire dying. Outside he put his mouth to my ear and spoke loudly: "Don't say a word, just run for the car." I was conscious now of a windlike sound, a roaring, though the night was so calm the smoke seemed to cling lazily to us in thin wisps. I followed him through the yard. We vaulted the fence (I remember his hands half throwing me over) and raced across neighbors' lawns, avoiding streetlights, to his car.

I gasped for air. When we reached the car the others appeared from behind trees, along a fence, jostling one another to get inside. I was last, and when I heard the engine start I hesitated, craning my neck to watch the orange peaks of flame rear up to the roof of the garage, retreat, and rise again. Even with the motor running I could hear the fire, a half block away, hear the windy sound like one long deep drawn breath, and a million muted voices crying out behind.

Greg grabbed me by the waist and pulled me in, and Billy shot off without the lights, running a stop sign and picking up speed. I burrowed, sobbing, into someone's chest, and felt myself shake.

Someone patted me, and then a scared voice said, "It was an accident." And another: "It was just an accident, you can't—" "There's no way—" "An accident, that's all—" "It's okay, it's okay—"

I must have been delirious. They couldn't be talking—how could I hear them if they were? For as far as we drove, with the windows rolled up tight, all I could hear was the deafening roar of the fire, howling voices in my ears.

7

It got dark early now, by five o'clock. The streetlights were already beginning to glow as I stood next to Madeline out back of her house. We didn't say much. Mostly we stared.

Only a few sections of wall remained standing. The charred wood uprights and fallen roof beams were almost completely black. The rest lay in clusters of waterlogged shingles and siding and seared fragments of wood. Exposed electrical cables twisted like tentacles. On the floor, bizarre trails of soot, permanently burned into the concrete, wound crazily. Near the old frame of the side door you could peer in and now and then spot shapes of warped metal beneath the rubble, and if you closed your eyes, you could reconstruct what they had been just the day before: garden tools, a stepladder, the handle of a lawn mower.

Still not talking, Madeline and I stepped to the edge of the doorway. The streetlights added their pale glow to the wreckage, and made it seem unreal. I scanned for some traces of the wall scrawled with Kevin's drawings. When finally I was convinced it was only sodden pulp, or buried beneath so much else it would rot before anyone could find it, I felt relief. Then the acrid stink of the ruins touched something at the bottom of my stomach. I straightened up, swallowed down the nausea, and for the first time in ten minutes, I spoke.

"What do they think caused it?"

Can a question be a lie? Mine was. Just about anything could be a lie, I saw, when a lie was your only way out.

"What caused it?" Madeline mimicked me, her voice shrill. "Sorry," she said. "I didn't mean that. I just thought it was obvious, Kerry. It was arson."

"Arson?" I tried it out, hoarsely.

"Somebody was in here. Something just got out of hand. They found—"

"Who?"

"The police. They found some beer cans, and—" All at once she fell silent.

"Beer cans and what?"

"Nothing. Just . . ." She kneaded her fingers. "Just ugly stuff. Graffiti on one wall. Insults . . ."

I forced myself to ask, "Insults?" just like a real friend would ask. "What kind of insults?"

"Things about Jews." I could barely hear her. "Things about me."

"And . . . where—where did—"

"They took it away. What was left of it, they covered it with plastic and loaded it into—"

We turned at the sound of footsteps. "Hey, stay away from there, you two," Madeline's father said sternly. I had almost never seen him when he wasn't peering over the top of a book, usually okaying whatever Madeline or her mother was asking him without drifting from his spot on the page. Now he was unshaven and his face looked drawn. His hands opened and closed uneasily. "I don't want you poking around in there. I'm not even sure the police are done with it."

Outside a wind picked up and I wrapped my arms around myself.

"Kerry," he said, "don't you have anything warmer?" He gestured to my sweater.

"I just threw this on and ran right over." That at least wasn't a lie. The phone call came from Madeline about three thirty. I'd been expecting something all day: a phone call, a knock on the door, ever since Billy dropped me off at home. Thank God my mother was asleep. I knew I stunk with the odor of smoke, so I crept down to the basement immediately, stripping off everything and shoving it into an old cardboard box. I stowed that behind the Christmas ornaments and tiptoed upstairs, naked, fumbling for an excuse with every step in case my mother greeted me at the top of the stairs. She didn't, and I made it to the bathroom. I filled the tub with the tiniest trickle possible so she wouldn't wake. It took hours, it seemed, until there was enough water for me to scrub the smoke smell away. With my skin rubbed raw, I tried to sleep. Ha. All I saw when I closed my eyes were the leaping flames. The next day my head hurt, my throat was sore. But still, no phone call. Not Billy. Or Linda. Or anyone.

Around noon, light-headed from not sleeping, I began to ask myself, Had it even happened?

When Madeline called, I knew the answer.

"I'm sure we've got a jacket somewhere for you," Mr. Abraham said, and went inside to look. Madeline was staring past one of the standing walls of the garage.

"The call came in the middle of the night," she said. "My dad wanted to go back alone, so we could stay for the competition, but my mother was still pretty upset; she thought at first it was the house that burned, and even when she knew it wasn't she was all shaky. Then we talked about my staying on, but there was no way I was going to concentrate on the project at a time like this. It's funny," she said, frowning. "I used to think I was tough enough to do anything. But Sunday morning all I wanted to do was come home."

With her dad gone into the house, Madeline inched back toward the garage.

"I don't want to go inside," I said.

"Come on," she motioned. "It's safe."

I watched from the doorway as she shoved at some charred boards. Underneath was a lump of misshapen plastic, a garish bright blue among the dark.

"Look at this," she said. Her tone seemed to brighten. "Do you know what this is? It's my pool. My old wading pool." She knelt down, tugged at one end, and pulled out what looked like a shrunken, solid puddle. "Remember this? Remember how we played pirates?"

"Uh-huh," I said, though I was looking at the spot where, the night before, Billy had held me on his lap.

"You'd think I'd know better," she said, "than to get upset over one stupid kiddie pool." I could hear tears in her voice as she spoke. I winced, and turned away.

At the edge of the flagstone walk that led to the garage I saw a dull glint of metal.

It was at the base of a row of shrubs. You had to be at just the right angle to see it gleam. When I took my first step toward it, the shining ceased, and for a moment I lost sight of it.

"Kerry?" Madeline called from the garage.

I stooped down and looked closer.

There, half-buried by dirt, was Billy's lighter. Where he had tossed it, I guessed, when it flared up. Or where someone had kicked it in our mad rush to escape. It was nothing you would notice unless you had seen it exactly from the angle I had, seen it by pure chance.

"Kerry? Where'd you go?" Madeline called.

I reached out my hand—drew it back—finally leaned down to fetch the lighter—

"Here you are, Kerry." I leaped in fright as Mr. Abraham draped an old parka around my shoulders. "Sorry," he said. "Did I startle you?"

"No," I wheezed, willing my eyes away from the lighter.

"Look at you, you're shivering." He gave me a tired smile. "You'd better take care of yourself, okay?"

"Okay," I said.

He went to chase Madeline out of the garage, scolding her gently, and I took another step toward the lighter. But she emerged so quickly, weeping quietly, I only had time to ease my foot over and press it down a little further into the earth. Then she was back, next to me. I gave her a tissue and hugged her as her sobs trailed off. I kept wishing each one was the last.

"Mad," I said. "What about your exhibit? Your equipment, and everything. Can you still be considered? Can you go back?"

"Impossible," she said. "It's over. Somebody won. They had to mark me a no-show."

"But you had an excuse." That triggered one ferocious sob, and I held her. "Okay. Okay. Don't think about it," I whispered. "Maybe there's some other scholarship you can—"

She pulled back to face me, her eyes tired and red. "Scholarship? Are you kidding? Kerry, I was thinking this could have been our house."

Once it had been fun to scan the halls for faces, my new friends' faces. Now I searched desperately, recognizing no one, as in some dream where I had to get somewhere but a crowd of oblivious strangers surged against me, all staring through me—

It was Monday morning. No one had called yet. I could understand. I was in dread of the phone, and I guessed they all were, too, as if the lines were tapped already and no whisper was safe anywhere.

I found Linda in the bathroom before history. We stood by the side of the sink and talked furiously, and every time the bathroom door opened and someone else came in we froze like thieves.

"I didn't come out of my room all Sunday," she said. "I told my parents I had a hangover. It was better to just get yelled at and grounded. A hangover they could understand."

"Linda." I couldn't keep it back. "They found it. The wall, the stuff that Kevin wrote."

"Oh, Jesus." She stared down at the floor, then said, abruptly, "It doesn't matter."

"Doesn't matter? All those names, and the drawing of Madeline."

"How can they trace that to Kevin?"

"Because—because he's so prejudiced."

"So? So a lot of people are." She glanced again to the door. "It's an ugly world, right?"

"But what do you think we should do?"

"Do?" Her eyes grew large and the lines in her face made her seem ten years older. "You're not thinking—"

"I'm not thinking anything, but *what should we do?*"

"First, calm down," she said, though she was the one whose hands were ice cold. "Kerry—we can't do anything."

All along, I realized, I had counted on someone coming up with a solution that hadn't yet occurred to me. "But can't we just—can't we—"

"*Can't* is the word, okay? Just think of that. We *can't* go back and undo it, right? We *can't* make it better."

"We're not going to just keep this a secret."

She put her hands to my cheeks and looked me straight on. "Kerry—we *can't* let this screw up our lives."

I swallowed. "How can you—"

"If it was something, I don't know, not as big—if we were just shoplifting, I'd say, okay, we just admit it. But there's no way admitting this does anyone any good. There's still a burned-out garage—"

"You should have seen it."

"—and a bunch of us with a record. A criminal record."

"Maybe not."

"A criminal record. You want that?"

"What I want is to be able to sleep at night."

"So do I."

"And not feel like I'm going to burst into tears every ten minutes. I can't even sit through classes. And I'm so goddamn scared. . . ."

"So am I."

"I thought, maybe if we tell the truth, we wouldn't be charged, and we could do something—to make up for it."

Linda was shaking her head already, as if to keep the thought away. "Make up for it? Kerry, what could you do? Use your *housecleaning* money?"

"We could think of something."

"Yeah, we could each have five years or so with a lot of time on our hands to do some thinking." I started to cry at that. "Listen. I know what you feel. And it's worse it's your friend. I know that." I was nodding now, just to the sound of her voice. "We all know that. But . . . we have to think, what's the best way out of this? For *all* of us. First of all, I'm sure they've got insurance. Did you think of that?"

I gulped down a sob.

"That's what insurance is *for*. For times like these. Nobody got hurt, and in six months there'll be a new garage, and we all—"

"We all get away with it," I whispered.

"We all get a second chance," Linda said calmly. "Why shouldn't we? You didn't light that fire. I didn't, either. We're not . . . we're not even guilty, really." She thumbed the tears away from my face. "Just be grateful for the insurance, that's all."

So the first cut of my high school career was spent crying in the girls' john, dreading the moment I had to step out into the halls where I imagined anybody could read my thoughts with one glance at my face. Later, when I found Heather, I felt worse. And with Greg, worse still. Like Heather, he didn't even want to talk about it. He wanted to whistle with relief through clenched teeth, roll his eyes upward, and mutter how all those newspapers were a firetrap, were an accident waiting to happen. But he didn't want to talk.

By noon I still hadn't found Billy, and by the afternoon I knew he hadn't even come to school that day. I suffered through the rest of my classes and then went to his house to find him. He lived in a big colonial that his dad's firm had renovated. I rang the bell, and when his face appeared, fleetingly, from behind a curtain, it startled me. He pulled me in, as if his mother, a hefty woman with a Peter Pan haircut, wouldn't even know I was there, but she had heard the doorbell and waved to me from the kitchen.

"Not long, Kerry," she called. "I want Billy up and at school tomorrow."

I said okay and followed him into the family room.

"Oh, Billy," she added, in a voice just a little too cheerful. "Don't forget that favor I asked you."

"What's that mean?" I badgered him as soon as we were alone. And then I saw his bleached-out face, as if the secret, like some parasite, had drained his blood. Billy was scared, no doubt. His cheeks, usually so ruddy and healthy, had the sallow look of pie dough. "What's that mean," I asked again, "about a favor?"

"Nothing."

"*Billy.*"

"I'll tell you, I'll tell you, just not—"

"Tell me now." But I didn't wait for his explanation. "Why didn't you come to school? Why didn't you call?" One question after another, so many he couldn't possibly have all the answers for me. But I kept on, shrieking at him in eerie whispers. I remembered old movies where somebody always stopped a hysterical woman by slapping her, hard. But Billy didn't have to slap me, he only had to say, "There was a detective here today."

I could hear the ticking of the grandfather clock in the corner, a disapproving *tsk-tsk-tsk*.

"The favor is"—he put his hand to his brow—"I'm not supposed to mention it to anybody. My mom doesn't want people thinking we're the type who get in trouble."

"A detective?" I stammered. "A *detective?*"

"He wanted to know where I was Saturday night. He was investigating a fire, he said. Just that. So if I could *account for my whereabouts Saturday night,* he said, he wouldn't *inconvenience* me—why the hell do they talk like that?"

"Because," I sneered, "not all their words have just one syllable."

"What's that supposed to mean?"

My words crept up in volume. "Where did you tell him you were?"

"At the 7-Eleven. Just hanging out in the parking lot. Till midnight or so. He believed me, I think."

"You think."

"I told him we were trying to get people to buy beer for us. You know, like I was admitting something."

"Who's *we?*"

"Well," he said, "I need to talk to you about that."

"Billy"—I turned away, though I could still see his reflection in the glass doors of a china cabinet—"you didn't mention me?"

"Kerry, I had to. He wanted to know who I was with. Who *would* I be with?"

Exactly, I thought.

"You, and Kevin, and Linda . . ."

"Oh, so you named them all, too."

"Damn right." He forgot about whispering and nearly shouted that one. "And you should be thanking me."

I turned. *"Thanking* you?"

"I gave you an alibi. So look, now you've got to cover for me. We were at the 7-Eleven, right?"

I nodded dumbly.

"I can still hardly believe it, a detective. She must have picked my name out of a hat."

"Who?"

"Madeline. 'Oh, here's somebody I don't like, Officer. Go look up Billy Stockton.'"

"They found beer cans," I said.

"Right, and I'm the only kid in this town who drinks beer."

"And they found what Kevin wrote. The Jewish stuff, and the swastikas. They took it away with them."

His face showed the struggle of furious thought.

I made a faint wave with my hand. "Billy," I said. "Why didn't you stop Kevin when I asked you to?"

"I know, I know, I should have."

He agreed so readily I could only murmur, "That's right."

"Because," he went on, "when you think about it, they could trace that writing back to us."

"That's why you should have stopped him? Because we could get caught? It doesn't matter *what* he was writing—"

"Keep your voice down—"

"It doesn't matter that we just stood around while he sprayed those words, while he—"

"No," he said. "That's *not* what we should be worrying about. Not now." He laid his hands on my shoulders. I pulled away. "We shouldn't . . . we shouldn't be worrying about anything. We should relax."

"Relax?"

"Because—he would have arrested me if he knew anything, really knew anything, wouldn't he? And he didn't. He just said thank you, and walked on out of here."

I felt like shaking myself, the way dogs do when they come out of the water, before I faced him again. He was trying his best to smile, but nothing was right about it, from the quivering lip to his eyes, blinking furiously. "Didn't he wonder about the way you look?"

"The detective?"

"Or why you didn't go to school?"

"Sure he did. You know what I told him?" He was proud of this, I could tell. "Food poisoning. I think he bought it, too. And my mom—my mom told him she wasn't feeling too good herself."

8

Like a butler, my mother stood just inside the door when I got home, but taking my coat was the last thing on her mind. Her face was locked up, the way it often looked, but she was biting her bottom lip; that was new, and enough for me to sense trouble.

"Kerry," she asked, "is there something I should know about?"

Is there ever, I thought, but before I could answer she said, "There was a detective here to see you."

"Oh my God."

She looked terrified. "Why 'oh my God'?"

But I was getting better at this. After the shock my face went right into its act. My brow scrunched up in puzzlement, but my brain shot ahead, like someone taking the stairs two at a time. So when the rush of panic started at the base of my stomach and worked upward, I wasn't just waiting around for it. "Because he saw Billy, too. It's because of Madeline's garage." I hung up my coat with complete nonchalance. "Well, a detective. That's good. That means they're going to find out who did it."

"But why does he need to see you?"

"Why do you think?" Better yet—keep myself cool, even

snippy, anything but scared. "They're doing an investigation."
I shook my head in annoyance. "Mother, sometimes—"

The doorbell rang. Good, another diversion. I turned eagerly to answer it.

There must have been certain ways a detective looked, and one of them was this: a tall man in an overcoat, hands in his pockets, his face so dull with boredom that later I couldn't remember a single feature, only a voice like a telephone operator on his eighty-seventh call of the day.

He nodded to my mother before he turned to me. "Kerry Dunbar?"

"Uh-huh," I whispered.

"Kerry, I'd like to ask you some questions." He held up a badge—it was all a blur to me—said his name was Detective Something—I didn't dare ask him to repeat it—and stepped into the hallway. "I imagine your mother mentioned I was here earlier."

I gulped and nodded, and followed him to the living room as if it were his house and he were ushering me inside. All I could think about was his sitting in his car somewhere, watching the house, watching for me to come home as if there were nothing else in existence that needed his attention more. To know a stranger was staking out my house almost scared me more than what he really was here for.

Almost.

My mother remained at the entrance to the living room. He gestured for me to sit down on the sofa. I did, but he kept standing, so I had to look up just to talk to him.

"Kerry"—he got out a notepad—"we're just checking up some leads on the fire at the Abrahams' on Saturday night. Can you tell me what you were doing that night?"

"I was with some friends," I said, trying to be so many things at once: innocent and sincere and concerned. . . .

"Billy Stockton?"

"Billy, that's right."

"Um-hmm," he nodded, as if everything were falling into place and so far I was doing fine. "Yeah, we were talking to Billy—in fact that's why we're here, he mentioned you were his girlfriend—so all we need to know is where you were, what time, that sort of thing. . . ."

It wasn't even a question, he made it sound so natural. It was more as if he had forgotten some of the information on his notepad and I would be doing him a special favor if I could help him now to fill it in.

"We were at the 7-Eleven," I said. "Till, I don't know, till midnight, I guess."

He didn't answer, just jotted something. His questions were casual, as if none of this were really important. Why were we there? he asked. Who was with us? I was pretty good, I thought. I forgot about my mother at the edge of the living room and even went along with the story of how we tried to get people to buy beer. The only hard part was, every time I finished, he would pause. Just look down at me with his pen poised, as if he were waiting for me to go on. It got so I dreaded coming to the end of my answer, so I offered him another detail or two, just to fill up the silence, and sometimes I had to gulp my words down just to keep from saying more.

"You didn't see Madeline at all, that weekend?" he asked.

"Just Sunday. She called me after the fire."

Again the pause.

I fought it, I fought it, and then I gave in.

"Uh, about Billy," I said.

His eyebrows rose. "Billy, yes?"

"I'm not his girlfriend."

He stared for a moment, digesting it. When he shut his notepad it seemed to free me from my statue's pose on the sofa. "Okay," he said. "You've been a big help." He thanked us and was almost to the door when he paused again. Both my mother and I thought he had remembered something, some last question, and I took a deep breath for what might come. In my head I replayed the conversation at high speed, probing for slipups—

But as quickly as he turned, he turned away, saying nothing, only nodding to himself, and he was gone.

Neither of us spoke. My mother stood watching the door for the longest time, which was fine with me. Because I was trembling, I realized, and I wondered if it showed.

At last she turned to me. "You're sure you told him everything you knew," she said.

"Uh-huh." And something I hadn't known.

I'm not his girlfriend.

"They check out everybody," Madeline said. "It's arson, remember. They've got to see who has it in for us."

"Great. So you think I have it in for you?"

"Of course not."

"Well, Billy then."

"I can't help that." We were up in Madeline's room. It was the first time in two days I'd talked to her. All the way over there, and even up the stairs to her front door, I didn't know what I was going to say. There was no way I could lie another minute to her, I was sure. I had to confess, I knew it. But the moment she answered my knock, it was as if some other girl took over for me. Someone much more used to lying. I was amazed how quickly *I have something to tell you* turned into *How could you do this to me?* Once begun, the lies spun out easily, and it seemed impossible that I could have acted any other way.

I sat on the edge of her bed. Madeline paced back and forth in front of me, but I glanced away whenever she neared the window, which looked directly out on the garage. "You want to know what the police asked? They asked for names of people we know who might have something against us. So I came up with Kevin Montrose."

"And Billy."

"I may have mentioned him."

"What a coincidence"—I wasn't faking, either, I heard real resentment in my tone—"you only name my friends."

"It is a coincidence. Kerry, I'm sorry, but the last thing on my mind was whether you count those people as your friends or not. You want to know what I was thinking of when I mentioned them? How, if you add up all the things they've said over the years, all the little comments, and slurs, and—"

"They don't add up to arson, do they?"

"They shouldn't, no!" she yelled. "But then some cop finds a drawing, a drawing of me so horrible I can't even stand to look at it—add that up."

"Mad." I let loose, and it felt good, even if I had no right to. "I'm trying to find out why a *detective* comes to my house—"

"I know—I'm sorry—"

"I'm just—I'm trying to be a good friend, and you're—"

"I'm sorry, Kerry," she cried. "I didn't mention your name. I didn't even think of you." I threw her the box of tissues, and she stood there holding them while her nose ran. "Do you know how scary it is? To think that . . . maybe whoever did it will be back? Can you understand that?"

I got off the bed, pulled a tissue from the box, and wiped her nose. "Sure," I said. "Sure, it's scary."

I felt her body heave against mine as she hugged me. "I need you, Kerry." She sobbed the words into my shoulder.

"I know."

I held her a little longer, till I thought she was calming down. When she pulled back, she smiled wryly and said, "Oh, great. Now I've got you crying, too."

"There's no reason," I sniffed, "that something like this should come between us."

When I left Madeline's, coming down the back stairs, instead of heading to the street I turned to my right. It was almost dark; I thought I could make it, just dart back there quickly without anybody glancing out a window. But while I was still in the shadows by the side of the house I saw someone standing a few yards back from the rubble, his hands deep in his pockets, gazing at it the way people ponder some curious exhibit in a museum.

He must have heard my shoes scuff on the walk. "Kerry," he called.

"Mr. Abraham," I said, flustered. "I didn't see you. It—it gets dark so early."

"Yes, it does." He motioned with a pained smile to the mound of ruins behind him. "But not dark enough, huh?"

I wondered if it was dark enough later that night, near midnight. I slunk my way back down the street to Madeline's house, sticking to the shadows of trees and fences. I surprised myself how fast I could move, stepping over crumpled leaves or gravel or anything that might make a sound, canny and high-strung as any stray cat on her rounds. There was no moon, and the nearest streetlight wasn't working. When I came to Madeline's house I crouched by the corner of her fence, waiting. When I was sure the lights were off inside her house and in the houses next door, I darted to her front gate. Opening it so that it wouldn't squeak took forever, and once past the gate, I was exposed. With only the rubble of the garage remaining, there were no shadows for cover, so I raced up the walk recklessly, knowing there wasn't a single lie I could manufacture to talk my way out of this if I got caught. Dropping to my knees where the flagstone walk led off toward the garage, I groped beneath the shrubbery and scooped through the dirt for Billy's lighter.

In seconds I had it. At first I didn't even stand up, I lunged to escape on all fours for a good twenty yards. Then somewhere in my flight I panicked, lost all sense of stealth, rose to my feet, and ran. I threw open the front gate—it must have screeched but right now I was faster than sound. Only at the end of a couple of blocks did I stop and try to compose myself. It would be hard enough to explain to some passing cop why a seventeen-year-old was out at midnight, harder still if the seventeen-year-old was doubled over, hyperventilating.

Against a tree, still cowering in the darkness, I thought of Madeline. Of the odds she might have seen me. Of the odds that I could pull it off. I was right, I thought, to do it this way.

For the first time I held the lighter up so I could look at it. The distant streetlight glinted on the surface. I saw the blond beach bunny, her hands back to fluff up her hair. If you stared closely at the face you could see how crude a drawing it was, how there was nothing to her, really, besides simple eyes, a nose, and a big, big smile. Nothing like a person there. She didn't get interesting, I remembered, until you flicked the lighter on and her bikini disappeared.

I turned the corner and started home. Tomorrow, I supposed, I would slip the lighter to Billy. . . .

I halted at the thought. Give it to Billy, and then what? Would his face still look so drained by then? Would he even realize what I had risked for him? Or would he just say, "Hey, my lighter, great"? How far along was he to forgetting?

And how far along was I?

How long—a week?—before Billy could light a cigarette right in front of me and I wouldn't think twice about the lighter?

I thought about how effortlessly I had lied to Madeline. I thought about my summer and my new friends; and seeing how a person could turn into somebody else so fast, I wondered what there was that couldn't change.

It scared me more than being caught to think that way.

There was a storm drain up ahead, just out of the glow of a streetlight. I could kneel down beside it, take one last glance at the smiling girl, and drop the lighter through the grating. I could wait until I heard the tiny, muted splash, and for the first time since Saturday night, I'd feel free.

Instead I thrust the lighter deep into my pocket, and with almost every step home I patted the bulge it made, checking that it was there. That was my part, to keep it. Even if the police would never find it, never connect it to Kevin's scrawl, I would know. I'd peek at it morning and night if I had to, I'd make it a ritual the way people kept candles burning in their windows, I'd do that and more, anything but let myself forget. I owed that much to Madeline.

Part Two

....

STAR QUALITY

9

By the end of the week I understood the code, which was, nobody wanted to talk about it. We were to go about believing that we had all been at the 7-Eleven that night. Linda was a natural at it. I envied her. Sometimes I felt I hated her, too, just for the way she could throw her head back and laugh at something silly, and only I, it seemed, would notice how her eyes stayed sharp and surveyed us all, wondering who was weak. Who might break. Soon enough Greg and Heather and Kevin had stopped those exaggerated sighs under their breath, stopped smoking any more than they usually did, and I wondered, did it work for them? Did they believe?

It didn't work for me. The following Saturday was the next-to-last home football game of the season, and I hid myself there instead of going to the beach to recycle trash with the Green Earth Club. But I didn't feel free of the fire for a second. All I knew was, as phony as I felt cheering play after play, I'd feel worse with the Green Earth Club, where everyone was so serious and committed, and where there was Madeline. That was the worst part of the week. How I'd avoided Madeline. Not purposely, but . . .

Somebody turned to me and said, "Billy looked good on that one."

"He sure did," I agreed, though I could hardly tell Billy

from the others down there. Then near the end of the first quarter Kyle West swooped in, his long wool overcoat flapping like giant wings behind him. He shooed some people over and wedged himself next to me. "Kerry Dunbar," he crooned.

I smiled and said hello.

"I see you didn't pass on any of my advice to Billy. He's still throwing those wounded duck passes downfield."

"That's mean," I objected. "I can't tell him that."

"Ahh." He nodded. "A really honest relationship."

"Cut it out," I scolded him. "We don't have a—a *relationship*."

"Oh, okay." He grinned. "So you can go out with me."

"I—what?"

"You heard me."

It wasn't long before one of those passes was intercepted, and the people in the stands slumped and moaned as one. Billy was the last man in pursuit of the Bedford defensive back who had picked it off, trailing him by five yards as he romped into the end zone, holding the ball aloft.

"Well," Kyle said, "if some college coach was watching, he could cross Billy's name off the list after that one."

"That interception wasn't all *Billy's* fault," I tried.

"No, not at all," Kyle replied. "After all, there were *wind currents* and *atmospheric pressure* and, oh, probably *gremlins*, and—"

"You're terrible," I said, laughing.

"Don't tell Billy," he said, mock fearful.

"Tell him? I'm not even sure Billy's *heard* of atmospheric pressure." We snickered together, about the only people on the Singleton side in a good mood.

"Hey," Kyle said abruptly. "Let's go."

"Go?" I said. "What do you mean?"

"Let's go. What's to keep us here?" There should have been a law to make guys with Kyle's eyes wear dark glasses.

"The—the game."

"Look." Kyle's arm went around my shoulders so naturally I just fell back into the warmth of his heavy coat. "Either Bedford's going to keep intercepting his passes, or we're going to stage this miraculous comeback. And either way, do you really care?"

I felt hypnotized. I started to say no, and caught myself. "Would you like it if I left a basketball game you were in?" I asked.

He rose, and I rose with him.

"You wouldn't *leave* a basketball game that I was in," he smiled. We squeezed past the people in our row toward the exit. "Would you?"

"Where are we going?" I sank back into the deep red leather seats of a silver BMW. It was his dad's car, Kyle said, and he didn't need it on weekends. To me it felt like a living room on wheels.

"Let's just cruise around. Listen to some music. Talk."

"You mean listen to you talk," I teased. It felt great just to get away. To Kyle I was hardly more than a stranger, but around him I felt giddy and free, and best of all: he knew none of my secrets.

We drove past some of the newer developments out on the edge of town, the BMW eating up the inclines and passing slower drivers without a hint of complaint from the engine; like Kyle, the car seemed perfect.

"Is this excellent?" he said. "Wouldn't you like to just pack up and take off in a car like this?"

"Uh-huh." I smiled, still marveling at all the lighted displays on the dash.

"You know, leave all your problems behind. Wouldn't you like that?"

"I'd like that"—I felt my smile falter—"a lot."

He set the cruise control so he could lean way back in his seat, stretch out, and steer with a couple of fingers resting on the bottom of the wheel. "Well, it's almost time. Time to take off and start a new life."

"Except—"

"Yeah?"

"You wouldn't care about . . . about leaving old friends, or—"

"Hey—when high school's over, it's over. Friends wear out, anyway."

"You're so sentimental."

"Think any of us will be friends in twenty years? Think that girl you're always with—that Madeline—think you'll be friends with her in twenty years?"

"Sure." I didn't sound too convincing.

"Uh-huh. Right."

"I *will*."

"Don't get me wrong. Senior year, I love it. Saturday afternoon. Great car." He turned to me. "Beautiful girl next to me."

"But when it's over," in a deep voice I tried to mock him, "it's over."

He barely noticed. He watched me and said, "Beautiful, *brilliant* girl."

"Kyle," I squirmed, "come on—"

"Valedictorian, right?"

"I don't know. That's a long way off."

Without a pause he pulled me to him and kissed me, hard, one finger of his left hand still steering while his eyes flickered away from me, to the road, and back.

"There," he said, letting me go. "That's sentimental, isn't it?"

I reached up, pulled the seat belt down around me, and latched it. "I—I don't know. . . ."

I needed time to take some deep, deep breaths. Don't be so awed, I urged myself. Talk back. But I felt as if I were at some high altitude where the air was thin. Then I saw the big green sign that marked the exit for the lake, and suddenly I wanted the lake, I wanted the Green Earth Club, I wanted people I had known for years.

I almost banged my hand on the windshield, pointing. "Can we get off here?" But as soon as I turned to him I knew I wanted this as well: the beautiful car, the guy from the *GQ* cover who couldn't take his eyes off me, the voice like a soft hand massaging my shoulders. I rose up in my seat, excited. Why *couldn't* I have it all?

"The lake? Sure," he said. "Might be nice."

I knew why not, instantly. I saw us slipping down a dune to the beach, where a cluster of kids would be searching diligently for bottles and cans. I heard myself, before we even reached them, begin to make fun of it all. Giggling, Kyle and I, and straining for straight faces.

And then I saw Madeline. As I strolled up, my arm in Kyle's, almost two hours late. I saw her face tighten up in disgust and heard her make some crack, Look who's here. What is it, halftime?

Worse, I saw her saying nothing. Not even meeting my eyes.

"No," I said to Kyle. "No. Forget it."

"You're sure?"

I took just a second to answer. "I'm sure," I said. "I like it right here. Keep driving."

I'd like to say that after the detective came to our house my mother was not herself. That she suspected something about me, no matter how natural I tried to act. The tense silences, the awkward dance when we met in a hallway and one stepped aside for the other to pass, all those were signs she wanted to know more. She was only afraid, like some parents, to pursue it.

But no, my mother had always been like that.

What would it be like, I mused, to have a mother who

would get in your face and demand the truth? The night the detective left, it was as if she didn't even want to be bothered. So I was wary, this night, when I noticed my mother smiling and humming songs to herself. It was ten o'clock and of course we still hadn't had our dinner yet, but she was handing me covered dishes and leftovers from the refrigerator with a sort of peppy grin. Over dinner I learned why. She told me that the big proposal she'd been working on for some time, a program for unwed mothers, was finally being considered by the county supervisor.

"That's wonderful," I said. "That's great."

She smiled about as widely as I had ever seen, and not that *ironic* smile, either. She explained how the program would help teenage girls with counseling and prenatal care and adoption agencies, even abortion and birth control information, if, she added, "the county doesn't chicken out. And," she added, "there's a good chance you-know-who will be named chief administrator."

"And you'd love it," I said.

"Um-hmm"—she smiled slyly—"I would." For a moment I let myself go and imagined her in this new job, enthused, involved—my God, *chipper*. I imagined her buying some new clothes, maybe even, big leap here, finding a boyfriend, or at least going out with some upbeat people now and then instead of those dreary friends of hers. I couldn't get over how *animated* she was, actually talking all through the meal, not just in spurts. All the time I kept agreeing and saying, "That's terrific," and once or twice, in a pause while she gulped her coffee, there was a big surge inside me that there were things I needed to tell her, and there might never be a better chance than this. There was Hank the Hunk, I could start with him. It was so long ago it wasn't even news. I bet she'd hardly blink. And then—and then if that went well, if I felt comfortable, maybe . . . maybe get to something—

"By the way, Kerry . . ."

"Uh-huh?" Something . . . a little more serious. . . .

"You haven't been to Ms. Trice's for a while."

I agreed. "I really have to get over there." I could start, I want you to listen, Mom, okay, and not interrupt—

"It's not even for the cleaning. . . ."

"Right." You won't believe me when I tell you but you have to let me say it all, you have to let me finish, or I—

"It's the reading she likes, and it only takes a half hour or so."

"I'll go this weekend." Because I'm scared, I'm really scared—

"Good." She stood to clear away her plate. "Kerry, can you do the dishes tonight? I've got two reports due tomor—"

"Mom?"

"Hmm?"

I watched her pour another cup of coffee. *You have to let me finish*. Right. What made me think I could even get started?

"Nothing."

"You're sure?" For a moment she looked as if she might sit back down across from me.

"Nothing. Just—Kyle asked me to the homecoming dance."

"Kyle?"

"That boy—I told you—remember—"

"Well, that's not *nothing*," she said. "That's very nice." But she was bored, I knew. And why not? It *was* boring, my little romance, when I thought of what I should have told her.

"I just . . . wanted you to know."

I cleaned a couple of rooms a couple of times a week for Ms. Trice, but the part I took the longest on was the part that probably needed it least.

"You even clean her basement?" Kyle had asked me.

"A basement room, really," I answered. "It was a darkroom once."

"Oh, *well,* that explains everything," he smirked.

I wasn't sure I could explain. How could I say, See, it's really *my* room. It has been for years, from the time I was five or six and Mr. Trice had let me watch as he worked on his pictures in the eerie red glow of the darkroom bulb. I was forever enchanted down there. He'd hum some old tune and poke with tongs at the paper in a developing solution. To me it was pure magic, and Mr. Trice a wizard. In my imagination the room became more than a darkroom. If I was angry at my mother or dad, it was a dungeon cell, and I a captive princess plotting my escape. The room was whatever I needed it to be, and I never even realized until now how much I missed it.

But I couldn't spend forever down there. There wasn't that much to clean, after all. Ms. Trice was upstairs, leafing through some chapter of hers, expecting me.

Just before I shut off the overhead light and left the darkroom I shut my eyes and caught my breath so there was no sound, and for a moment I could have been seven years old again. With nothing more to worry about than getting caught down there by Mr. Trice, or getting home late for dinner. I smiled; it seemed funny to think that once we even had a dinnertime at home.

I reached into my bag, sifted through the tissue and keys and lipstick until I felt it. Solid, square, cold, unmistakable. Nothing that ever belonged in my bag, nothing you could associate with me. I wasn't even going to look at it—especially not at her dopey smile. The smile she always wore, the one that could mean anything, even *I didn't know I did anything wrong*. You couldn't help but forgive her, she was so cute.

I clenched the lighter in my fist, and with my other hand pulled open a cupboard and felt way, way back, past the mason jars and coffee cans, to an old cigar box full of clutter, old pens, and matchbooks. I rooted my fist down into the box, let the lighter go, and stepped back, swinging the cupboard shut, shaking my hand as if I had dipped it into a slimy pond.

I didn't feel any better, of course. But it was where it ought to be. My worst secret, in my most secret place.

If Ms. Trice was miffed that I had taken too long, or that I hadn't been over in more than two weeks, she didn't show it. She had a chapter ready for me the instant I stepped into her sun porch, and in no time she was chuckling along as I read.

But I must have sounded weary, or maybe just preoccupied, for somewhere in the middle I sensed she didn't seem near as amused. At the end of the chapter I asked, "When do you want me to come over next time, Ms. Trice?" When I looked up I found her watching me.

"Well, Kerry—are you sure you want to?"

"Of course I do."

"Don't agree so quickly," she cautioned with an upraised finger. "You'll get yourself into trouble that way. It just seems you've been . . . reluctant, lately."

"I know I didn't get over last week, but I've been so busy."

"I understand that. You're a senior now. I'm sure there's not always time."

"No, I want to come over." There, how did that sound? "I'll be in . . . how about Wednesday? Four o'clock?"

She waited a few seconds. "You don't have to make an appointment."

"I'll call just before I come, how's that?"

"I might not hear it. You know I turn this damn hearing aid off half the time when I'm alone. No, Kerry. Just come over. The doors are always open."

"You know, Ms. Trice, I always wondered about that. Why—"

"Why an old lady living alone doesn't lock up her house?"

"Well, yes."

"If I'm going to get robbed, so be it. No sense their ruining the locks while they're at it. Hell, they could be living in the basement for all I know. I haven't been down there for more than a year."

"There's no one in the basement," I said, and we laughed at how serious I sounded. "I take special care of it."

"I know," she said. "Anyway, if I locked my doors, how would you ever have slipped downstairs so much when you were a little girl?"

"I—" I squinted at her. "You knew about that?"

"Your sneaking down into Russell's darkroom? Of course we knew. We used to hear you, back before my ears went bad, playing down there."

"I always thought I was so . . . *secretive*," I stammered, embarrassed. "I never touched any of Mr. Trice's equipment. . . ."

"We know you didn't," she said. "That's why we never stopped you." She reached out and ruffled my hair. "Sometimes a person just needs a refuge. We were pleased you chose us."

It took all the charm at Kyle's command, and that was a lot, to coax me to my first party after the fire. Just the thought of Linda, Kevin, Heather, and Greg, together again, not in the safe halls of school but the way we were when we started out that night—a little drinking, a little restlessness—it all set me trembling. Kyle knew nothing, and it was awkward sometimes. At one point I ended up with Heather and Greg and a few other people, and our mouths talked gossip and school, but the eyes of the three of us shared something else. Another time I watched Linda carrying on with a group, but as soon as she saw me across the room she ducked away and appeared at my side, as if none of us should be left alone.

I knew then it wasn't a case of who I *wanted* to be friends with—what choice did I have? Compared to what I shared with them, it was as if there *weren't* any other kids than we six; as if, except for Kyle, those who hadn't been in that garage were just children, really. Like small-town cousins who'd gawk and stammer if you ever showed them what the big city was really like.

No, we were stuck with one another.

Even Billy. I was stuck with Billy, though there were times I could barely stand to look at him. Homecoming came late that year, in the middle of November. At the dance I watched him braying at his own crude jokes. We had lost the fourth game in a row that day, and I might have felt a little sorry for him as his season toppled around him if he hadn't haunted the edges of the crowd, slipping outside where he must have had some beer stashed, returning to ask a different girl to dance each time. With Kyle beside me in his tailored black suit that showed off his height and lean build and made him look so sophisticated, I could recognize Billy in all his ugliness.

"He's pitiful," I said to Kyle during one of the slow dances.

"Aww, he's not so bad." I noticed now that Kyle and I were going out he wasn't nearly as hard on Billy. "He's just not at your level."

I smiled up at him in the dim blue shadows of the gym. "Are you?"

"Of course," he laughed.

"You're so con—"

"Hey. How many times have people looked at us tonight?"

"I haven't really noticed."

"Oh, of course not."

"All right. I have. But that's because I'm Kerry Dunbar, nice girl and good student, and they can't believe I'm with Kyle West"—the truth was, *I* still couldn't believe it—"dashing, *conceited* athlete."

"You didn't say good-looking."

"Okay, that, too."

"Well." He laughed. "You're almost right. They're not just looking because of me. They're looking because we make a *knockout* couple. A *magazine cover* couple."

"Kyle, you're—"

"Because we have star quality."

For a moment I laid my head on his shoulder and just felt him guide me, gently drifting to the song. I opened my eyes.

"Star quality," I said. Across the room I could see Billy loading up a glass of punch and watching us. "I like that."

After homecoming, college fever spread through the senior class like a virus. Miss Tufts, my guidance counselor, took a whole period of my English class just to explain the application process. Although she must have been fifty, she always dressed as if she were an eight-year-old at her first piano recital. "You know, Kerry," she said when she stopped at my desk, "I've just the place for you. Have you ever thought of applying to Ridley?"

"Ridley?"

"It's a Near Ivy, you know." Miss Tufts was always referring to schools as "Ivies," "Near Ivies," and "the Rest," and the worst thing an AP student could do was even consider one of "the Rest." "Come by my office and we'll chart a course."

Once I was there, carefully turning the pages of the glossy catalog, poring over the color photos of the red brick buildings, the multicolored hillsides in autumn, I could feel my heart pounding faster. It all looked so dignified, and elegant, and . . . it was like some secret that the world kept from you as a kid. Adult life, that's what it was. It started somewhere like Ridley. My mouth went dry. It was how, I saw, you forgot things you needed to forget, by going somewhere far away. . . .

This was my way out, I saw, under the cool fluorescent lights of Miss Tufts's office. I had heard of Ridley. It was one of those schools people mentioned in the same breath with Vassar, Radcliffe, and others, exclusive and—I slumped, dejected at the sudden thought—expensive.

"Your grades," Miss Tufts continued, "would put you high on their list."

It's not a question of grades, I said to myself. It's my mother. To be fair, it was the price. Schools of that kind cost more than twenty thousand dollars a year. Long ago my mother had sat me down and confided that there was no way I could expect to go to any school more expensive than the state university at Atherton. And now I walked home from school, toting the Ridley catalog which Miss Tufts said I could borrow overnight, resenting the hell out of my mother.

At dinner, just after ten, I mentioned it. "I think I'd like to go to Ridley," I said.

She took a sip of coffee and eyed me sadly over the rim of her cup, as if Atherton were the last of the things we had in common. "Is your father sending you there?"

"I thought, maybe Dad can help. . . ."

Major error. That started my mother on a ten-minute tirade about Dad's financial irresponsibility, and the next day I returned the catalog to Miss Tufts. "I don't think I can consider Ridley," I told her. "Even if I have the grades. I don't think we have the money."

She rose up in her chair. "Kerry Dunbar, I don't want to hear that *defeatist* attitude in you." She shuffled through the pages of a thick folder, murmuring to herself. I stared up at the glass-enclosed map of the United States mounted behind her desk. There was a colored pin, either gold or brown, showing where each of last year's seniors had gone to school. When I was a freshman I had always meant to ask why gold and brown, when the school colors were blue and white. By the time I was a junior I had the color code figured out. I guess I should have been flattered that she had a gold pin all reserved for me.

"Tonight," she said, "when you write to Ridley for an application, be sure to ask for the financial aid information. Mention some of these scholarships." She photocopied a list for me with such confidence that, though I walked out of the guidance office browsing through the information, what I was really seeing were the deep green shadows of the campus, the ivy-covered—

"What a brain," Billy accosted me as I stepped out the doorway. "You even read in the halls."

"No," I said, startled. "It's just—"

"College stuff, huh?"

"Yes, Billy. College stuff." Of course he didn't catch my tone. "What about you?"

"Oh, I don't know. I guess I'll go to Renfield." Renfield was a little college about two hours to the north. In the world of Miss Tufts, it was definitely brown pin all the way. He shrugged a laugh. "I can sneak in, I guess. It's only Renfield, you know. It's not, like, Harvard."

"That's right," I assured him, and turned to go. "It's only Renfield."

"Kerry."

There was something in his voice that caught me. He drew closer. The way his eyes jittered back and forth made me uneasy. "Billy, what?"

"I never told you, but . . . that night—you know . . ."

"I know which night, Billy."

"I never found my lighter."

He looked at me. I swallowed, deliberately. "So?"

"So? So, where is it? It's got to be *somewhere*."

"We shouldn't be talking about this." And then I couldn't help myself and answered him. "Don't worry. It's somewhere. It's in your car."

"No it's not."

"Or you kicked it away when you ran, or it *melted*. How's that? Just let—"

"Or they got it." I could barely hear him. "So I've been thinking . . . maybe it wouldn't be so bad . . . if we went . . . maybe it wouldn't be the end of the world if we turned ourselves in."

"Turned . . . ourselves in?" I managed.

"Did you ever think about it?" he blurted. "You know, going to them before they came to us?"

"No."

"*No?*"

My God, this was how it would happen. After all our secret sighs, Billy would be the first one to crack.

I looked down at the Ridley forms in my hand.

"Of course," I seethed. "I never *thought* about it—and I'd never *do* it. And don't *you* do it."

He glanced over his shoulder again. "Just, sometimes I think, it'd be for the best. . . ."

He went on from there, but I heard little. I was listening to what I'd say when the police came around.

I wasn't there, I say. Yes, I know Billy gave you my name.

I see me lead them, then, lead that detective next door to Ms. Trice's. I dig out the lighter and lay it in his palm.

What really happened, I tell him, is I found it the day after the fire, at Madeline's.

At least that part was true.

But why did you keep it? I hear the detective ask. Why did you cover up for him in the first place?

He—lied to me, I say. He told me he was never there, somebody borrowed the lighter that night.

Then why would he tell us you were there, too?

Because, I say without a pause, he's afraid to take responsibility.

Someone took his lighter and burned a garage down, and gave it back. And you believed him?

I nod. I guess it shows, I say, you never really know what some people are capable of.

"Kerry." Billy was waiting for an answer.

I felt something harden inside me then, and that was all it took to look him straight in the eye and say, "Billy, you can't tell. None of us can tell." I held his glance for ages, it seemed, until he nodded. He understood.

"You're sure now. You won't do anything. If you feel like you're going to, you come talk to me again."

"Okay," he wheezed.

I smiled, to reassure him, but really I was thinking of the lighter. How it wasn't just a souvenir, something a little more solid than a conscience. If he really went to the cops, it was all I had to save myself. It was survival.

"Ridley!" my dad crowed at the dinner table. "My little girl, off to an impressive school like that."

"It's not as if I've been accepted there yet. . . ."

"A mere formality."

My dad was the total opposite of my mother: if our house was gloomy and somber, his house had all the lights on and the stereo booming, even when he and Lynn, his third wife, were separating. He had married almost immediately after he divorced my mother, but the marriage to Claudette didn't last long. Whenever he slowed down and began to choose his words carefully, I knew he was on a story that must have had Claudette in it and he was deciding how he could tell it without mentioning her. I wondered, now that he and Lynn were divorced, would he do the same to her?

With Lynn he had had two daughters, Zoe and Joan. Dad insisted I call them my "sisters," and after he corrected me enough times I began to do it naturally, even though there were twelve years and two marriages between us. But the more Dad tried to make me a part of their family when I would come down to visit, the less I felt like one. I was probably most comfortable when I could just drop in (he lived about an hour's bus ride to the south), stay a night or two, and slip away without a lot of fanfare, or hugs, or the family photos he was always arranging. It sounds terrible, but in a way I was relieved when I learned he and Lynn were breaking up. My last few trips down before they separated were full of stiff conversations that died out like campfires made with wet wood, and so many slammed doors and clanging pots I came away with a headache.

"It's better for everyone this way," he once said, talking about his latest divorce. "A guy like me—I should really just play the field."

"Play the field?"

"Sure. See what's out there. Test the waters."

"Dad?" I asked. "Why is it a guy always talks about his love life as if it's sports?"

He chuckled. "Good question."

"'Play the field. The ball's in your court. Get to first base. Strike out.' Women don't talk like that."

"Maybe," he said, "it's because with sports . . . men at least *think* they have a chance."

This visit went as fast as all the others. He had started therapy. What a change it was making, he bragged, and talked about it all weekend. Honesty, that was what he'd been running from all his life. Knowing himself. By Sunday afternoon I was confident enough to bring up college, and he was delighted.

"But Mom said Ridley was out of our financial range."

"Hah!" Dad yelped like a dog with its paw caught in a door. "Your mother just doesn't understand money, Kerry. She looks from gas bill to mortgage payment, and not a bit beyond." He leaned across the table and lowered his voice, as if we were in a crowded restaurant instead of the tiny kitchen of his new apartment. "Kerry, a kid like you can be anything. And you can go anywhere. Especially to a school like Ridley. You know you can, don't you?"

I was slow to say yes, but I wanted to, despite seventeen years of my mother saying no.

"When you get home tonight I want you to fill out that application form. I want you to send it right off."

"I already filled it out," I admitted.

"There you go. That's initiative."

"But I need to ask you for the application fee."

"The what?"

"To apply. There's a fee."

"Oh." Dad looked distracted. "Oh, of course." He laughed. "That just shows how long it's been—"

"It's forty-five dollars," I said quietly.

"Yikes," he said, and flinched. It was supposed to be funny, I thought.

"I could ask Mom, I guess. . . ."

"No, no, don't you go bothering your mother. She—she wouldn't understand any of this." He sat up straight, hearty and confident. "What's forty-five dollars"—he shrugged, getting out his checkbook—"when you're reaching for a star?"

I watched him sign the check with a flourish.

"There. You and I, kiddo, we're the dreamers in the family. But at least we're honest about it, right? We can confront the truth."

He slid the check across to me. "Thanks," I said. And then, impulsively, "Dad"—I looked at him—"as long as we're . . . *confronting* things . . ."

"You have to in this life. You just have to."

"There's something else I need to talk to you about."

"Well, shoot," Dad said.

"What would you tell . . . a friend"—already I felt the urge to back away, so I hurried my words before I ran dry—"who did something . . . really wrong, and got away with it, and now wants to make up for it?"

"A friend?" My dad's mouth was set in a grim line. "Are we talking about you, Kerry?"

"No." I took a second too long to answer, I thought. "No, we're not, Dad."

"Good." He leaned back, relieved. "In that case, does your friend really want to go through with this?"

"I—I don't know."

"Because to that I'd say, 'Don't do anything you don't want to.'"

"Don't do anything—"

"You don't want to. It's a tough lesson. It's knowing your-self, like I said. Knowing what you really want, deep inside. You say your friend got away okay? And everything turned out okay in the long run?"

I nodded. "In the long run, I guess."

"Then I'd say to this friend, 'Hey, don't rock the boat.'" He shrugged, and smiled, and so did I; for a moment it was all so logical.

Then I asked, "And what would you say if it were me?"

For a moment he looked alarmed, but I held my smile, and he knew I was only saying, *Just suppose*. "I'd probably tell you"—he grinned—"to go ask your mother."

11

By late December basketball season was well under way. This had meant nothing to me for years, and now meant everything. It was afternoons hanging out at the gym watching practice and seeing how many times Kyle waved to me in the stands. It was Kyle in that skimpy little uniform, his long legs bare and muscular. It was a profile of him in the local newspaper and nods and high fives as he strolled through the halls. For him and whoever happened to be with him, which was, as much as I could manage it, me.

Sometimes after a game we'd sit in the diner and go through the moments of the game. One night he scored thirty-two points, and even though we lost you couldn't tell it by the rowdy bunch we sat among. Everyone wanted to tell Kyle how good he had been, and he couldn't finish a sentence without someone new coming up and saying "Nice game" or "Way to go."

But at our crowded table he and I were always a little island of confidence among our noisy friends. It was perfect. And it had been perfect for almost two months. Our dates weren't just dates, they were ... *events*. It wasn't as if he didn't know *exactly* how to charm me to death—he certainly did. But he made it all seem so casual. Cruising in his father's BMW, stopping by his house. The first time we went over there I met his mother. She was pretty and athletic-looking, and she seemed to see right through Kyle and be able to deflate him with no trouble. "Kerry, just remember," she teased as she took me on a tour of the house. "Don't believe a word he says."

"Oh, but I have to." I smiled back at him, and said, loud and sassy so I was sure he heard me, "After all, he's such a celebrity."

The house was huge, with six bedrooms, a Jacuzzi, a pool, and a wall of stereo equipment. "Kyle's father is a lawyer," she pointed out. "He's gone about three-quarters of the time." She laughed, and added, "Which is probably why we have a good marriage." I chuckled knowingly. Around her, I felt comfortable, confident. I could join her in ranking on Kyle; we'd team up and accuse him of being conceited, lazy, even dumb.

But without his mother there—which was the next way I saw the house, in the evening, the two of us alone on the burgundy leather sofa with his arms around me—I didn't feel quite so confident. Sometimes when Kyle would kiss me I had to shake free glimpses of a pickup truck's cramped front seat on a sweltering August night. In those moments I caught my breath and reminded him I had to get home.

"Sure," he always said. "Of course."

He'd walk me down the flagstone steps to the BMW, his arm around me and a wry little smile on his face, as if I were the one missing out by wanting to leave. And maybe I was.

For Christmas he gave me a photograph, blown up to twelve-by-sixteen and framed in oak: the two of us dressed for a fancy date. Kyle looked absolutely stunning, and I looked . . . flustered. I looked good, I guess—Kyle insisted I did—but the flashbulb had left faint red dots in the center of my eyes, and I reminded myself of a startled deer, caught in the headlights of a car. Once I showed it to Jessica Oliveri—she hadn't been to a single Green Earth Club meeting since I had stopped going—and I thought she was going to cry. "It's so beautiful," she gasped. So I felt silly having reservations, and I hung the photo over my desk where I'd see it all the time. Someday, I knew, I'd get used to it.

"A condom?" Kyle pulled back to see me better in the golden afternoon light of his living room. "You've got to be kidding."

Oh, to just say, Yes, yes, what a little joker I am, instead of stalling him with a barely audible, "No, I mean it."

His hand fell again to my thigh. "But why a condom? You're on the pill, aren't you?"

"Uh . . . not right now. . . ."

"Well, why don't you just go on it?" He kissed me, and as I took my hand from his wrist to touch his face, his hand slipped further up my dress. "That would take care of everything."

I pushed him away and took a deep breath. "Not exactly everything. . . ."

"What, then?" he whispered in my ear. He ran a strand of my hair through his fingers.

"Kyle," I said. "I—I have to get home."

He pulled back. I felt his gaze all over my face, and I dreaded what he'd say next—

"I'll drive you," he offered.

"Drive me?"

"Sure—if you really have to go."

"I do," I said. "But no, thanks, I'll—I'll walk. I need the exercise."

I need the oxygen, I should have said. I trudged home, watching the icy puffs of my breath as if recalling fragments of our conversation. Once again we didn't do it, despite all of Kyle's deft maneuvering. And we didn't *talk* about doing it, which was what I wanted. It was the word *condom* that caused the problems, but it could have been *safe sex* or *AIDS* just as easily. He'd think I was joking and I'd have to convince

him I wasn't. By then the mood had always changed, at least
my mood. And, I had to admit, it wasn't just a fear of AIDS
that scared me off from going to bed with Kyle.

He never got mad. He never, like Hank the Hunk, acted as
if I were lucky even to be with him. But still, every time an
evening ended, no matter how tenderly he kissed me good
night and chuckled at the way I'd work free from his grasp, I
couldn't help thinking, What if this is the last time? What if
he just gets tired of me, always saying no? I'd feel myself
tremble and my stomach grow weak. But then he'd call me
up, or surprise me outside a classroom, and I'd feel safe
again. Once, out of nowhere, Miss Tufts mentioned what a
nice couple she thought we made, and when I wondered how
she knew, she said, "Why, Kyle told me." I was proud to know
he was even telling teachers about us.

"Of course I told her," he teased me later. "I needed a
good college recommendation from her."

I began to wonder, did *anybody* really talk about safe sex,
the way they say you should in those public health ads? I
needed to talk to someone. There was Rhonda, but letters
to her were ancient history by the time she wrote back, and
I couldn't see saying all this on the phone—not in my
house.

Maybe, it occurred to me, I could try Madeline. . . .

"Listen to this," she said one afternoon up in her room. "I
read where there's one kind of ant species where all the males
are bred with tiny brains, and their sole function is to have sex
once, and only once, just to keep the population going, and
the females don't let them do anything else, not work or raise
their young or anything that they could conceivably screw up.
They just let them have sex that one time, and then the males
die." She paused and looked over. "Now, what was it you
wanted to ask me?"

"Never mind."

"Never mind? You don't call me for about a month—"

"Two weeks, not even. Only since midterms."

"And then you"—without warning her voice lost its shrill-ness—"how come you haven't called me?"

"I—I've been busy."

"Busy with that *guy*. Prince Charming."

"Because of Kyle," I was quick to agree. "That's it." But Kyle wasn't the reason I hadn't called her. And Kyle wasn't why I rushed off after the classes we had together, instead of waiting for her by the door. But Madeline didn't press; she was absorbed in her number-one college choice. "It's on the list of the top ten radical schools in the nation. Kerry, I'm surprised you didn't even *apply*."

I saw, out her bedroom window, that most of the rubble of the garage had been cleared away. "I told you"—I turned back to her—"I was hoping for Ridley."

"Ridley? Yuck, barf, gag."

"Cut it out. It's a good—"

"It's a good place to join a sorority and network yourself into some dumb, socially useless, high-paying job before you marry some rich—"

"Mad!" I yelled at her. "Stop being so nasty."

"I'm just—"

"You're just putting down everything I say. Kyle, and Ridley. What's next?"

She didn't answer. "I also applied to Atherton," I said, "just to be safe."

"Atherton's okay." It was as close as Madeline got to apologizing. "I'll probably go to Atherton myself, if we don't get some kind of scholarship. My number one costs a fortune."

"There's no chance"—my voice sounded high and thin—"you could still qualify for that science scholarship? Are you sure there isn't some—"

"*Kerry.*" I flinched. "Let's just drop that, huh?" She

shrugged. "Atherton's okay." She nodded to herself. "At least Atherton's *real*."

"Get this," I heard Linda's voice on the phone. "Heather told."

"Heather . . . *told*?" That was how well trained I was; I knew better than to even mention the fire. "You're kidding."

"Yeah." And suddenly she started giggling. "She told it to a *priest*."

"A priest?"

"Can you believe it? Heather? Did you ever know she was so religious?"

"Linda," I almost shouted, "how can you *laugh*?"

"Because she told him in *confession,* that's why." But I was still confused, and she could hear it in my voice. "*Confession,* Kerry. The priest can't tell anybody what you say."

"Oh," I said. "Of course. But—"

"And she hasn't gone in years, she told me. Can you see her in there, kneeling down? Probably had to go through a few hundred other sins before she even got to the fire."

"Don't *joke*."

"I can think of a few she—"

"Linda!"

"Kerry, relax. A priest can't tell anybody. It's between him and her."

I said hoarsely, "You forgot God."

"Oh, right," she said, and giggled again. "Well, I'm pretty sure God's not going to tell. So it's really just the priest we have to worry about—and a priest has to die with all those secrets."

"So—"

"So we can't live with one? Relax."

I tried to. She helped me; she got me thinking of Heather in the confession box, dying for a cigarette, and calluses on her knees from being there so long, and the priest probably dozing off before she even brought up the garage. And when I felt better, even started to laugh, we talked about easy things, clothes and teachers and music. It was just what I needed. Though I never got around to Kyle, at least I could tell Linda about my mother, like what a nag she'd been lately, and Linda didn't have to rush in and tell me how bad her mother was, too; she listened. She let me talk. And when I said how my mother was still after me about staying out late ("You know I'll be at that conference next weekend for my unwed mothers project, Kerry. I don't want you at some party half the night. I want you home."), only then did Linda interrupt.

"Your mother's going to be away next weekend?"

"The county board wants her to look into this proposal she made—"

"That's fantastic."

"Yeah, it's nice for her. She works really hard—"

"No, it's fantastic that she's going to be away. Think of the potential."

"She made me promise I'd stay home."

"Exactly. Think of the *party* potential!"

I was slow taking it in. "Party?" I gulped. "You mean, here?"

"How many times does she go away for the weekend?" Linda asked.

"Well . . . never."

"There you go. This is your chance." I could feel the excitement in Linda's voice. "It's a blessing."

12

By Tuesday people were coming up to me in the hall asking how to get to my house . . . by Wednesday Billy told me he would arrange for the keg . . . by Thursday people were talking about the party as if it had *already* happened, a landmark social event . . . and by Friday I could hardly think, I was so scared.

Really, what were the chances of some stray spark igniting another blaze like that Saturday night back in November? Still, gather up all the ashtrays, smoke detectors, and fire extinguishers that I might, I couldn't relax. Who said that this time it would be a fire? I knew now how parties sprawled into mobs by midnight, how people changed after too much to drink and the first thing to go was the better parts of them.

All week kids called to me in the hall for directions and I felt the phony smile take hold of my face. "Stop by," I'd say, the merry hostess, insides cramping up with dread. Of course, I never mentioned it to Madeline. She hated parties, anyway, I reassured myself. And the last thing I wanted was for her to see me with Kevin or Billy or Greg.

Around seven o'clock Saturday night Billy and Greg lugged in the keg, immediately taking turns squirting beer right from the spigot into each other's mouth. "Just testing," Billy said, laughing.

By nine or nine thirty there was a big crowd in the living room, and it really wasn't my party anymore—it was a thundering, smoky, pulsating thing that seemed to live on its own. Once in a while someone pulled me in to dance. I did my best to be a part of it. I flung my arms and whirled and shouted into people's ears, the music was so loud. At the kitchen table the quarters gang was at it. Jessica sat before a shot glass. Her pale skin was flushed, and her makeup, which was maybe a bit too thick, shone in the harsh kitchen lights. "Great party!" she called to me, and proudly held up a dollar's worth of quarters.

I squeezed past a couple making out in the hallway, and paused for a second at the edge of the living room. Out of all the people, the dancing acrobats and the guys on air guitar, the overturned chairs, the cloud of cigarette smoke, out of all that chaos, my eyes went right to Kyle. He stood at the edge of the dancing crowd, not quite a part of it, but swaying naturally to the music. He held out his hand to me as if I were in an evening gown, descending some grand staircase, and I kissed him. "Fashionably late," I teased.

"I tried to gauge it so I'd be just in time for Kevin Montrose smashing beer cans on his forehead. Did I miss it?"

I pulled him into the huddle of dancers. "We held it up just for you."

Later, one after another, the kids congratulated him. With the season nearly over he had already been named to the all-county team. Word had gotten around about some of the scholarship offers he had received. He answered the questions and shrugged casually at the raves, his chin up and his eyes direct. With his arm resting gently on my shoulder I could listen to talk about point guards and baseline moves all night. For the first time in a week, I felt a little bit at ease.

Just then I heard raised voices from the living room and ducked back. If I thought the dancing was rowdy before, now some of the jocks had lined up on opposite sides of the room and taken off their shirts, and Billy, Kevin, and others from the football team were yelling out "Fifty-two buck right!" and "Twenty-five red tail, on *three!*" It wasn't until they huddled in the middle of the floor that I began to catch on.

"Guys," I called. "Wait a minute."

"Break!" they shouted, and two scaled-down lines formed head to head. Guys pawed at the carpet like bulls. There wasn't room to dance now, anyway, so the rest of the crowd stood along the walls and cheered, just like at a real game.

The first play was a quarterback sneak, and Billy rammed into three or four defensive players. There was a big pileup in the middle of the room, and I thought that they might just do that a few times and get tired.

"Let's go, Singleton!" I heard Jessica's screechy high voice from the door to the kitchen.

The teams lined up for another play.

Kyle's arms came around me from behind and I turned to him.

"Can you believe this?" I moaned. He nuzzled my ear.

One of Billy's beer can passes ricocheted off the arch to the hallway and clattered on the floor.

"Kyle, can't you—can't you stop them?"

"Let them go," he said. "They'll tire themselves out."

"Who cares if they're *tired?*" I turned to him.

"If they're tired, they'll leave earlier." He drew me to him and kissed me, hard. "And we can have a little time alone."

I nodded uncertainly.

He put his hands at my waist and pressed me against him. "Now your mom's away tonight, right? For the whole night?"

"For the weekend," I conceded.

"So"—he cupped my chin and kissed me—"we'll just wait."

I heard an explosion of laughter and a high-pitched screeching, then a snarling, a spitting. I peered through the raised cups and beer cans of the spectators and saw my cat

Mitzie held aloft. She swiped at Billy with her claws, but he handed her over to the boy who was playing center. "On *two!*" Billy yelled, and the center lined up, both hands pinning Mitzie to the floor.

"Let her go," I shouted, but with all the cheering I might as well have been praying.

The crowd chanted, "Pass—pass—pass!" I had a vision of Mitzie hurtling through the air like a punctured balloon. But instead Billy handed her off to his running back, and I saw Mitzie's claws sink into his stomach so that he twitched and leaped as if he had touched a live wire. Then she kicked off, flying through the air, fur on end, until she landed on the sofa.

"Fumble!" somebody shouted, and eight guys dove for Mitzie on the sofa, slamming into one another until she worked her way free underneath and scrambled off. A second later a sharp *cr-a-ac-ck* filled the air, and the sofa collapsed under their weight, the two front legs shooting out like shrapnel.

"*Oooohhh*," people called, and from others came a mocking cheer, and I stood there, among them all, not knowing what to do. The guys climbed off the sofa. A short tussle started. I wondered about Mitzie, I wondered about the sofa—and I wondered about the crowd. For everyone began to dance again as if there were still hours left to enjoy themselves, and not a one of them had to face my mother.

A couple of guys tried vainly to reattach the front legs to the sofa while others danced around them. I watched from across the room. Finally one of them came to me and mouthed, "I think the frame is broken."

I felt a tickling on my face, and when I realized my cheeks were slick with tears, I hurried through the kitchen out to the deck in back, and started sobbing. It was freezing outside. The sweat turned cold on my body, and then the shivers began. Through the window I saw kids in the bright, warm kitchen, still clustered around the table with their shot glasses. As I watched from the deck, I saw Kyle saunter into the kitchen. He leaned down to the group at the table and said something. He smiled. Somebody tried clumsily to give him a high five. Then he went back into the living room, and the kids at the table, first one, then a couple, got up. Soon the kitchen was empty, except for a straggler or two who tried the empty keg or peeked into the refrigerator. My hair, so damp from sweat five minutes ago, now crinkled with frost. Another boy wandered into the kitchen, and a step behind him was Kyle. His arm snaked around the boy, and he whispered to him. The boy grinned, nodded knowingly, and the kitchen was deserted again.

From out in front a couple of cars started up, and the voices from small groups rang through the frigid air.

Kyle came back into the kitchen, opened the door to the basement, and called down. Then he glanced out onto the deck.

I shrank back into the shadows.

When he left the kitchen I hobbled down the steps of the deck and into my backyard, as if to escape. I couldn't sneak back inside. All I wanted was to be alone, but Kyle would find me wherever I hid, and the thought of having to *hide* from him made me burst out in tears once more.

I thought of telling Kyle that. I saw him nodding, humoring me, saying, You're absolutely right, running his hands through my frozen, spiky hair—but this time, not leaving. No matter how many times I asked him to.

And rather than face that, I crept through the darkness and the patches of snow on the ground, and when I got to the fence between our house and Ms. Trice's, I tried to climb it as I had when I was a six-year-old. But I was wobbly and ungraceful now, happy just to stretch out a foot and touch down in her yard.

I swore I could hear Kyle's voice, calling for me.

Her basement door was unlocked, of course. I inched it open and slid through. Past the laundry room was a narrow corridor, and halfway down on the right was the old darkroom. I could barely recognize the shapes of Mr. Trice's equipment on a shelf along one wall. It had never seemed this black all the times I had come here. I stretched out a hand to get my bearings. Somewhere, I imagined, there was still a little girl hiding. It's me, I wanted to say. Listen to what's in store for you. But I knew no little Kerry would have anything to do with someone like me, sweaty and wretched and reeking of cigarette smoke.

I crawled up onto the old tattered sofa bed in the corner and huddled in a musty afghan. The shivering eased, and I shut my eyes and lay perfectly still, waiting for sleep.

Waiting. I heard the ticking of my watch. The slam of a car from the street.

I scrunched myself around. Lay on my side. Wadded up some old towels for a pillow. Turned onto my back. Took long, steady breaths, deep as snores, hoping my body would take the hint.

Then I opened my eyes and stared at the ceiling.

I thought I knew the room well enough, even in darkness, but I surprised myself. It took forever to find the handle of the cupboard, grope among the jars, the rags, and finally lift the lid of the cigar box.

In my grip it seemed bigger than I remembered. Heavier. I even tried to flick it once, but the flame didn't catch. Hunched over on the edge of the sofa bed, I pressed it against my forehead and felt myself shake.

Do it quickly. Go back, pick up the phone. Just confess. Just do it all *fast*.

Then maybe this room wouldn't seem the way it did, a way I couldn't stand: like an ordinary basement room with a musty smell, and nothing more.

But all I did was put the lighter back on the shelf and

reach, still shivering, for the afghan. How nice to think one simple phone call could convert the room to magic once again.

Too bad I needed more than magic.

When I awoke my head throbbed like the pulsing of a Don't Walk light. My skin felt slimy. My hair was matted to my neck. I was nauseated, but dying of thirst.

I slunk carefully back to the house and found the eerie silence of a battlefield, the day after. Six thirty on the kitchen clock. I cringed. Four and a half hours sleep.

And about a hundred hours of cleanup ahead.

The empty keg floated in a barrel full of icy water. There were blotches on the kitchen linoleum, dented beer cans and plastic cups full of cigarette butts on every available spot, and the sofa—

The sofa. I fought back tears. It looked crippled, like one of those beggars in a Charles Dickens novel. There was a burn mark on one of the cushions. The detached legs lay nearby.

Tufts of Mitzie's fur were scattered about the carpet.

With every glance I saw something else that was broken or stained.

I thought that, with luck, there would be heavy traffic, and my mother wouldn't get home until six.

And then I called Madeline.

It was a miracle for her even to come, but soon enough I realized she was going to make me suffer, and she didn't have to say a word to do it. She just fumed and sighed and rolled her eyes and shook her head and muttered almost inaudible comments to herself, until finally I confronted her.

"Why did you come over if you're just going to be this way?" By this time we had scrubbed most of the kitchen floor and dragged the keg to the backyard.

"Because I'm your friend," she snapped.

"Then act like it." I wiped my brow. My hair felt like the dirty strands of a mop.

"I'm going to." She laid down a wad of sooty paper towels and faced me across the living room.

"I really need a lecture," I said. "That's just what friends are for."

"I'll tell you about friends, Kerry. Item A: without any questions they give up a Sunday that they should be studying for an AP bio test—"

"Oh my God, I forgot the test is tomor—"

"—to help a friend, an old and trusted friend—"

"You don't have to stay much longer."

"—but that's okay, because of Item B: they don't mind that they weren't invited to the first party their best friend has had since, I don't know, since eighth-grade graduation, but that's okay, too, because from the looks of this place, it was no event that any *environmentally responsible* individual would want to attend."

"That's why"—I sounded pitiful—"That's why I didn't—"

"Which brings us to Item C: friends trust in the friendship enough to say what I'm going to say. What's with you, Kerry?"

I chanced a breath. "What do you mean?"

"You know what I'm talking about. Ever since the fire you've been different."

"How?" I asked. Then almost eagerly, "Tell me."

"Okay." She took a deep breath and so did I. "You walk through the halls at school and every time someone says, 'Hi Ker'"—Madeline mocked a nasally greeting—"you just about *drool,* you're so pleased that everybody knows your name. You drop out of the Green Earth Club, you go out with a neo-Fascist football player—"

Absentmindedly I tucked a beer can into the garbage bag.

"And," she shouted, "you don't even recycle your cans!"

I waited for more—but that was all. And when I dared a

glance at her, I saw only her chubby short legs, her frumpy black sweater, her thick hair messed and stringy with sweat. Sitting there like Buddha, generous enough to share with me the Perfect Truth of who I was, when really, she didn't have a clue.

She thought I didn't need her anymore, not with all my wonderful new friends.

It was sad to see how much she valued me. To see how wrong she was. For the first time in my life I felt sorry for her.

"Then," she said, "you have this storybook romance with the most insincere, most manipulative sleazeball this school has—"

"You mean Kyle West," I said coldly. Suddenly, cleaning the entire house by myself didn't seem that major a chore.

"You know exactly who I mean."

I said it calmly, without a trace of arrogance. "I'm in love with Kyle West."

Madeline let out a great snort of contempt.

She stayed another hour, and in all that time we didn't say a word, except once when she pointed out some broken glass and asked me where the whisk broom was.

Part Three

THE ASSASSIN

13

....

The sofa lay at a permanent slant on the carpet. If you tried to recline on it the jagged end of some broken slat poked you in the butt. So you could sit at one end of it or the other, but not in the middle, unless you were Mitzie.

"Well," my mother said, staring long and hard at the wreckage. "It was an old sofa."

"I'm going to pay for it," I said, "with my housecleaning money from Ms. Trice."

"Don't waste the money, Kerry. I just can't see bothering with it." That was about all she said for a week. A week of brooding, tense silences. Of meaningful sighs. Of the door slamming when one of us arrived, and an echo lasting for hours.

Actually it was a week like most weeks in our house.

I watched Madeline, about half a lap ahead of me, bounce along the perimeter of the gym in what passed for her running style. Miss Chappelle, the phys ed teacher, stood in the center and blew shrill, regular blasts on her whistle, the way you train dogs. We had been pounding in endless circles for the whole period, the stale indoor air burning down our throats.

Madeline's hair flopped all over, her T-shirt was eight sizes too large. Every couple of steps she reached down to hike up her shorts, but it didn't interfere with her running rhythm—she had none. She only had a puffing, nose-in-the-air expression, like some basset hound determined to swim for shore. Once I would have snickered, seeing her. But it had been more than two weeks since I had even talked to her, and I wasn't about to ruin things by laughing.

"You know what we ought to have?" I panted, coming up beside her.

Several steps later, without turning: "Are you talking to me?"

"Mad"—the words burst out in annoyance—"who do you think I'm—"

"Save your breath, you'll need it," Miss Chappelle crowed.

"You know what we ought to do?" I tried again.

"No." Three or four gasps later: "I'm dying to know."

"Don't be like that," I said.

"Okay." And with that she started to pull ahead. In no time I found myself ten feet behind and forced myself to catch up to her.

"That's right, Dunbar!" Miss Chappelle hollered. "Pick up the pace." I guess it was encouragement.

"Mad, listen." I tried to look at her as I ran, and almost got tangled in somebody's legs. "You know how, in health, when we talk about AIDS, half the kids still make jokes about it?"

"Yeah?" Pant-puff-gasp-hack. "So?"

"Well, why don't we do something about it?"

"Good idea. I'll work on a cure tonight."

"I mean it."

"What could we do?" she asked. And just so I wouldn't take it for granted that she was even speaking to me, she added, "And when would somebody as popular as you ever find the time?"

"Stop it. I thought, why don't we have an assembly?"

Nothing. But at least, I noticed, no sneer. I hurried on. "You know how the principal loves assemblies."

"Those are different," she panted. "Those are for the football team, or—"

"But look, he might go for this. We get a speaker, and information. Or a film. There could even be questions from the kids. . . ."

By now she was running in a slow shuffle. "Well"—the breath labored in and out of her—"maybe you've got a point."

"It would be great, if we worked hard at it. Get the kids to talk about"—I tried to sound casual—"oh, safe sex, and . . ."

"It's what they need," she said.

"That's what I mean."

"Because they don't take it seriously."

"That's *right*." We turned and faced each other on the track, jabbering excitedly. The other kids plodded past us. "We could tie it in with health class—"

"And make sure," Madeline said, "some reporters are there—"

Three whistle blasts resounded through the gym, deafening me. "Abraham. Dunbar. Get moving. Once you start," Miss Chappelle bellowed, "there's no stopping!"

I made my face gritty and determined, but I was smiling inside as Madeline and I willed our legs to push us on. We managed some kind of pace. It wasn't fast and I had no idea how we'd ever finish our laps, but at least we were running together.

"In New York City," Madeline said, "the schools *distribute* condoms."

"Do they?" the principal, Mr. Kendall, asked politely. "I may have heard something about that."

"And here you don't even want us to say the *word*."

"Uh, Mad." I put a hand on her arm. "Maybe we could dis-
cuss—"

"I don't know how we're going to do an assembly," she
seethed, "if we can't even use the right words."

"She doesn't mean that," I said.

In Mr. Kendall's office we sat in the twin chairs before his
vast desk. Up until this year I had never had much to do with
him. He was always roaming the hall, cornering some athlete
and asking about his "game face." Madeline and I called him
Mr. Ken Doll, since his slicked-back hair looked a little like
molded plastic, and the smile that never left his face made us
think of Barbie's boyfriend. Every September he had an assembly where he welcomed the kids back to school, and to
the freshmen he would say, "Nice to have you on board," as if
the high school were one big happy boat. This year, since he'd
seen me with Billy, and then Kyle, he had even started talking
to me. I had to admit, sometimes it was fun to just relax and
laugh at his dumb jokes. And it came in handy here; at least
he gave us a few minutes in his office. That was step one. And
the first time we mentioned AIDS and he didn't blanch and
shoo us out the side door, well, that was almost a victory in itself. But every step beyond, I knew, would be delicate.

"Madeline means that we think the kids can be trusted to
act responsibly. . . ."

"Kerry, I can say what I mean."

"It would be," I continued, "a real learning experience."
Ken Doll's eyebrows rose at the phrase, and I knew I had said
something right. I went on; I told him we could get help from
organizations.

"What kind of organizations?"

"Health organizations, *county* health organizations who
could supply speakers, and information, and maybe we could
get a discussion going, or have a panel . . ."

"And who would be on this panel?"

I told him we didn't know yet, we could find out, I babbled on just to keep Madeline, who was starting to fume beside me, quiet. And suddenly I sensed what to say: "There's one thing I do know, Mr. Kendall."

"And what's that?"

"I know we'll go over every step of the assembly with you first, to make sure it all checks out."

As if we had made a secret agreement to ignore Madeline at that point, neither Ken Doll nor I reacted to her exaggerated sigh.

"Well," he mused. "If you get a few more details to me, we can consider it. How's that?"

"That's great," I said.

"But about this speaker . . ."

"Uh-huh?" I looked at Madeline. She was full profile to Ken Doll now, staring out his window.

"Whatever he says, he'll have to understand, the official school policy on this subject is abstinence."

"Abstinence," I repeated slowly, as if it were a foreign phrase.

"Abstinence. We'll be able to get that message across?"

Madeline grumbled, "I didn't know the school *had* a policy on AIDS."

Ken Doll answered as if I were the one who had spoken. "Oh, we most certainly do, and the policy is abstinence."

From the corner of my eye it looked like Madeline was twitching. "Then that's no policy at all," she said.

"Abstinence, sure." I nodded. "We can do that. No problem."

"Kerry!"

"Good." Ken Doll smiled. "I'm not exactly saying yes, you understand, I need to think this through—but I suppose we could even arrange for an honorarium for your speaker. Say, oh, fifty dollars, subject to approval."

"That's great," I said. Ken Doll shook our hands heartily and ushered us out, and all the time Madeline didn't look at him once. She didn't even look at me.

"Why do they call it an honorarium?" I whispered.

"Because they want to pay you as little as they can get away with."

I watched her stomp off, past me, past the secretaries, and head for the hall. She doesn't even appreciate this, I thought. She doesn't even understand what I'm doing for her. I called her name.

She turned, her eyes black. "What?" she snapped.

I knew then I could plan a thousand assemblies, from here to graduation, and I could never make up what I owed her.

"I like the way he has you trained," she said.

"He doesn't have me trained."

"What's next, jumping through a hoop?"

I almost said to hell with it and left her there, but the assembly, I told myself, was worth it. I'd do my part. So what if it could never please her.

At least it would look good on my record.

Maybe good enough for probation.

"Let me get this straight . . ."

"Kyle . . ."

"You hid in some neighbor's *basement*?"

I had run into him in the cafeteria, emerging from the lunch line with a tray full of food.

"You actually *slept* there?"

"Kyle, we've been going over this for *two weeks*."

"Okay, okay," he said. "Kerry, I'm just kidding you."

"I know." Every time he brought up Ms. Trice's basement I laughed with him how silly I had been, and every time I figured that would be the last I'd hear of it. It never was. He wasn't even mad that I'd avoided him. I wondered if it even occurred to him just why I'd fled next door. "I've just—I've been having some problems with Madeline."

"Yeah?" Both of us heard it then, the table of guys clamoring for him to sit down with them. "Really bad, huh?" he asked, but I saw his eyes creep up, over my shoulder, and I knew he was eager to join them. He took half a step in that direction, and before I knew it I was telling him about the AIDS assembly, as if the rush of my words could hold him there. My voice chirping like a frantic parakeet, I reeled through the whole scene in Ken Doll's office before I noticed he was smiling.

"What?" I asked. "What's so funny?"

"Nothing," he smirked. "Just—still on that condom thing, eh?"

"No, no," I hurried to make clear, "I didn't mean anything . . . you know, about us." I took a quick breath. "I thought you'd just want to know about the assembly because it's—it's important to me."

"Well," he said. "I do." His eyes slid past me, to where the guys, all rowdy, were calling his name.

"Oh, go ahead." I gestured to his friends. "Male bonding time."

"Thanks, Ker." He leaned over his tray to kiss me. "Hey," he said. "This assembly. I want to hear all about it, okay?"

"Okay." I watched him saunter to the table until I realized how conspicuous I must have looked, standing there in the middle of the cafeteria. I ended up in the lunch line, moved along the way a pebble gets caught in the surf, thrown up the beach, pulled back, flung up again.

"Oh, man, that must have been *so-mm-me* party," a voice boomed up ahead of me. "Why wasn't *I* invited?"

I turned to see Teddy Mattson tapping a conga beat on his lunch tray. He wore a tie-dyed T-shirt and a Boy Scout cap.

"I"—I had never really said much to Teddy—"do you mean—"

"I mean your party. I heard about it." He suddenly motioned to the utensils rack. "Wow!" His jaw fell open in excitement. "Clean silverware!"

The lunch lady kept asking for his order.

"Just the macaroni," he said.

"You gotta take the whole dinner," the lady said, handing him a plate.

"The burger, too?" He sounded wounded. "You're *forcing* red meat on me?"

I stared at Teddy.

"I know," he said, "you didn't invite me because you don't know me and I'm weird, et cetera, and I don't drink—"

"No. Just I don't know you."

"You don't think I'm weird?" He sounded disappointed.

"Mmm."

"No, that's okay." His face beamed a goofy grin. "Really, that's okay. It's all an act. I'm really as normal as you."

I glanced around. If he became violent, would *anyone* come to my aid?

"Here, you want my meat?"

"*What?*"

He stabbed his burger with a fork and dangled it over my tray. "High cholesterol. Senseless animal slaughter. Plus it tastes like cardboard." He flicked his wrist and the burger plopped onto my plate.

"No, really, I—" I got mad. "Take this away."

"You should eat it. Or at least something. You're getting thin."

"I am not, I just—"

"I know, you shed a few pounds this summer. But deep down you still feel fat, right?"

"Not exactly fat, just—" *Why was I saying this to him?*

"So how many pounds did you lose?"

"It's *none* of your business."

He stepped to the cashier, slowly sorting pennies and nickels from a collection of coins, beads, Bazooka Joe comics, and Cracker Jack toys he hauled out of his pocket. The kids in line muttered impatiently.

"All right, all right," Teddy said to me just before he bolted from the line. "You win. Next time *you* can buy me lunch." Then he dashed off, making beep-beep noises. I stared down at his gray, lone burger in the center of my tray.

"What'll it be, dear?" the cafeteria lady asked.

I snared the burger with a fork and maneuvered it into the trash. "Just a salad," I said.

14

"Come on," Kyle said. "I'm worth a detention, aren't I?"

I shrugged.

"Kerry, forget the class—"

"It's not class I'm—"

"You're such a good person."

"No I'm not." I knew he was just teasing, but it set me off. He had talked me into cutting Ethics in Government for him, just to walk in widening circles around the edges of the school lot. "Don't say that."

"You are. And everybody knows it."

"Nobody knows it. Nobody knows me." I looked up at him. "You don't know me."

"Oh, right. Like I don't know you."

"You *don't*. There's a lot—"

"I know you never even thought of turning Ken Doll down."

"—that I should tell you—*Ken Doll*?"

"Right. Once he asked you, I'll bet you never even—"

"Why didn't you say you were talking about *Ken Doll*?"

"Hey, lighten up. What else would I be talking about?"

"Never mind," I said.

"I was just saying, you never thought of turning him down, because you're a good person."

"I'm a sucker, you mean."

"Well"—he feigned innocence—"you could look at it that way."

Only a sucker would have let herself get cornered by Ken Doll that morning, the way I had.

"Kerry, Kerry, Kerry," I remembered his hearty voice booming up the stairwell as he prowled for smokers and graffiti artists. "Just the lady I was looking for."

Madeline used to seethe when people called us *ladies* instead of *women*. "Hello, Mr. Kendall."

"Listen—I've been thinking over your proposal. Like it. Like it a lot. Ninety percent certain, I'd say, that we could do it."

"That's great. Well, I have to get to—"

"Important issue," he said.

"It is."

"It got me thinking . . . with energy like yours, and ideas like yours—you know where you would really be a big help?"

I shook my head.

"Somebody like you ought to be on the Senior Prom Committee."

"The Prom Committee?"

"Absolutely. With someone like you in charge"—already I was in charge?—"we could make this year's prom something *special*—something to *remember*. And," he confided slyly, "it'd be quite a feather in your principal's cap. What do you say?"

"Mr. Kendall, I didn't even *go* to the junior prom."

He brushed it aside. Meaningless.

"I don't know how much good I could do—the prom's in May; it's already March. . . ."

He chuckled condescendingly. Such modesty.

"I'll . . ." I knew there was no escaping it. Not if I wanted the AIDS assembly. "Ninety percent certain," he had said. Which was probably just one Prom Committee volunteer shy of *yes*. "Okay," I gave in.

"You're a natural," he said with a grin. "Plus, you're already part of the perfect couple for the prom, right? Mr. All-County and Miss National Honor Society."

Tell him it's *Ms.*, I thought. Not *Miss*. Do it for Madeline. But I only said, carefully, "You mean Kyle West."

"So you might as well make sure the *evening's* perfect as well, right?"

"Uh, of course . . ."

"If you want a job done right—"

"Do it yourself," I murmured.

"That's my little lady." He smiled.

Now a cold, sleetlike rain had begun to fall, and in minutes Kyle and I were both soaked.

"My problem is," I complained, "I can't say no."

Kyle took my hand and pulled me to him. "That's funny, you don't have any problem saying no to me."

He kissed me, and I held him till the cold rain trickled down my neck. My socks squished as we walked. I started to sneeze.

It couldn't have been more romantic.

We wandered the limits of the parking lot one more time, just talking. Talk with Kyle never really seemed to go any-where, and sometimes after we were together I couldn't even remember what we had said. But I was used to that by now. I guess I even liked it. When you talked like that, after all, you never got too near those places deep inside that you didn't want to know were there. Still I'd think there were things he had to know. But it was easy to back off; stop nagging, I told myself. Stop acting like your mother. It felt so warm with his arms around me, there was no way I would ruin it with words.

"Let's go out tonight," Kyle said. "My mother complains I don't bring you around enough."

"I can't." I let out a colossal sigh. "I promised I'd help Jessica plan her party."

"Oh, that's right," Kyle said, "it's tomorrow night. I can't believe she waited a whole month after you had yours." In less than four days Jessica had left about a dozen messages on my mother's machine, begging me to help her. Now, as the weekend approached, I was getting frantic worry notes tucked in my locker all through the day.

"I don't mind. I like her." Like her or not, a nudge more from him and I would have told Jessica anything to get out of it.

"Well, I'll just see you at the party, then. I'll stop in later."

"When things are at their peak." I smiled.

"Of course." He grinned back.

By ten o'clock Saturday night Jessica was roaring drunk. Each time she returned to my side she giggled something more and more incomprehensible, and then screeched with laughter at her wit. Her pretty auburn hair hung in damp strands. I watched from the edge of the crowd, trying to pick up and clean up and replace—early on a lamp had crashed to the floor—but soon I gave up and started watching the clock, waiting for Kyle.

It wasn't long before I found myself clustered with Linda, Billy, Greg, Kevin, and Heather. Nobody said much. We smiled, sipped our beers, looked away. I was almost getting used to it, at party after party, the point when the dancing and the drinking games lost their appeal, and we all ended up with one another, standing in awkward silence.

"Hey." Kevin's meaty hand patted my shoulder. His round, fat face was slick with sweat. "Kerry, what's this I hear about an assembly?"

"What assembly?" I swallowed.

"Yeah, I heard something, too." Linda leaned over. "It's about AIDS, right?"

"AIDS?" Billy stepped closer. "We're having an assembly about AIDS?" He looked at Kevin and they started snickering.

"I don't know—"

"I thought," Linda said, "you were in charge. I heard Ken Doll say that." Her brow wrinkled as she remembered. "You . . . and Madeline."

The name was enough: I felt their curious stares as they stood in a half circle around me. Even Billy and Kevin stopped their fag jokes and looked on. Linda was no longer puzzled now—just wary.

"No." My mouth was parched, but I couldn't even raise my beer to my lips without shaking. "No." I was careful not to meet any glances as I spoke. "It's just Madeline."

I thought it was obvious, my lie, but Billy just grunted, "That Madeline. Can you *believe* her?"

At the mention of her name our eyes all turned to him. For a second nobody moved.

"What—what do you mean?" I asked.

"Just, that's *so* like her." He was drunk, that was it. Then he gulped his beer and crumpled the cup, and little by little I felt the group stir around me.

Billy went on. "An *AIDS* assembly. She's never at something like this, right? At a *party*?" And as he rambled on, stumbled over his words, I saw them loosen up. For even I couldn't deny it; it was different hearing her name sputtering out of his mouth, so different from the months and months of avoiding it, like some curse. It wasn't fear I sensed from them, but actually . . . relief. The relief of getting away clear. "You know where she is? She's probably home *studying*. Like it'll kill her if she doesn't get an A."

While Billy took a swig of his beer, Kevin Montrose snorted, "Jews are so smart."

No, not relief. It was far uglier, and I shrank back.

"Smart, and rich," Billy added.

"Just watch," Kevin said, without a thought of caution. "The new garage'll be even bigger. Two stories. Full of Mercedes."

"They don't have a Mercedes," I said. "They have a Toyota." Nobody heard me. I tried to say it louder, but it was too late. Billy had launched into a joke, something about a Jew and an Irishman, a tavern and a bank. I couldn't follow it; I only saw stiff necks and limbs unwind in a frenzy of giggling. At the punch line beer spilled from cups held by shaking hands. Billy stamped his foot gleefully; he had another one. "So there's this rabbi and a priest, right? And they're in a lifeboat. . . ."

Soon everybody was hysterical. I looked around at the shining faces. No, I thought, stop it—

But I was laughing, too.

Hesitantly at first. Then harder, and soon, giddily, helplessly, no different from the rest. When one or two of us calmed down, somebody else got us started again, and we rumbled on, laughing raucously, contagiously. There was an ache in my side as I gulped in breath. Heather brayed like a donkey for air. Greg rubbed away the tears, so did Linda—

So did I, though I wasn't laughing any longer, I realized, as I felt my chest constrict and force out a sob, and by the time I looked up, frightened that the others would notice, I saw their faces change, too: their eyes hollow, their skin white, the smiles gone except for Billy, until his too collapsed and his true face peered out, scared, one step from panic.

We fled from one another. I took shelter in the kitchen, where there was no one to see me but a couple making out in a corner, so I didn't even try to stop myself. I let my body heave with the sobs. I saw my fingers shaking.

From there I staggered through the living room, past the dancers. Up close, there was face after face that I recognized. Several called my name. I stopped for nobody, my hands to my eyes.

When I reached the front door I saw him, loping casually up the walk.

"Kyle." I ran down the steps and dug my fingers into his

back and held him tight, sobbing against him as if he were my last chance.

"Hey." He stroked my hair and kissed me. "What's the matter?"

I shook my head. "Get me out of here," I whispered.

He nodded and cradled my head. "Okay." We kissed again. "Where do—"

"I don't care," I cried.

"Well," he said, "we could go to my house."

I just held him tighter.

"Is that okay?" he asked, his arm around me, already easing me down the walk toward his car. "It'll be quiet. There's nobody home."

I didn't say yes exactly. I just stopped saying no, and with Kyle, that was enough.

15

From late Saturday night to Monday morning there were long stretches where my feet didn't once touch the earth, fuzzy dreams where I'd stare out a window until my eyes watered over, rooms I'd walk into and forget why, pass into another and remember, return and forget again. I spent hours in front of the mirror, not really looking at myself, just waiting for the person staring back to nod and say, Yes, it happened, yes—

I'd feel his arms around me as if he'd never let me go.

His breath in my ear, his kisses—

But sometimes . . .

Sometimes I'd crash in free-fall the way a plane dips in an air pocket. And then whatever room I was in felt way too small, airless and gray. I'd race outside and gasp for breath, and then panic, hear myself choking, my heart beating—

It wasn't even the fire. Through it all I didn't think about the garage, not once.

Instead, I'd hear things he said.

"Aren't you glad?" he had asked.

"Um-hmm." I snuggled closer.

"I was thinking, whatever happens, you'll always remember me. Even years from now. I like that."

I didn't say anything at first, it sounded so romantic. It

didn't later. It sounded as if he were way ahead with his life and already looking back at now. *Remember* me? Who wanted to be remembered? But at the time I only said, "I'm glad you like that." I knew it was stupid to sleep with somebody and not use protection. I also knew how hard it was to say no. Why talk at all, when I could hear his heart beat against mine?

But later, in my memory, the words were louder than the heartbeat, and to get past them I'd concentrate hard on something nice: his strong arms, the small, delicate lobe of his ear, just *feeling* and not thinking. Soon enough I'd soar again, roam through my house like a ghost with a beautiful secret. But each time I never got back up quite as high, quite as fluttery and moonstruck. By Monday morning I needed to see Kyle as soon as possible. *Needed to* more than *wanted to*. There was a difference, and I didn't like it.

What I got instead was Billy Stockton, ambushing me after phys ed, when I was tired and most vulnerable. I tried to brush him off and keep going, but he followed along next to me with jittery, furtive steps. "Oh, are you going my way?" I asked at last, and I meant it to be sharp. That was the first time I really faced him. He looked gaunt and weary, as if he hadn't slept since the moment his last joke at Jessica's turned sour.

"Kerry, you know, I was thinking . . ." The hall was crowded and he was standing a little too close beside me.

I snapped, "Speak up." Big mistake.

"I was thinking, uh, about the prom. . . ."

"*What?*"

"If you—if you and Kyle . . . aren't . . ."

Suddenly I was more interested. "What about me and Kyle?"

"Like, you know, at Jessica's . . ."

"What about Jessica's?"

"You were there alone, right? I didn't see Kyle. And later, you were all upset—"

"*We* were all upset as I recall."

"But people said you were crying, and, I thought . . . well . . . if you guys aren't together anymore I thought, hey, why don't *we* go to the prom?"

I stared at him.

"You know," he said nervously, "you and me."

I watched his face: bloodless again, perspiring, not far at all from the way it was at Jessica's. I was going to say, Why do you *think* I was crying? but I knew better than to mention the fire. I didn't have to. It raged inside him still, even here, and I wondered how long he could stay so scared and not have something snap.

I remembered the day he caught me outside Miss Tufts's office: *Maybe it wouldn't be the end of the world if we turned ourselves in.*

He would do it, too.

I knew then I'd say anything to keep him quiet.

Even yes.

"Sure," I said. "Okay."

It stunned us both. But my mind was racing ahead.

"You mean—," he mumbled.

"Sure. Why not?"

It was crazy to stand here and chat about the prom, two arsonists in tux and gown. I had no intention of going with him, I would *die* before I went with him.

I was going to stiff him.

Say yes, keep him quiet for now. And later, when maybe his urge to confess wasn't quite so strong—stiff him. How easy it would be. Didn't he gulp down anything I offered him? *Billy, I'm sick. I don't think I can go.* Or better yet, *Billy, I have to go with Kyle. You know how much he needs me.*

Stiff him. A thousand reasons why rushed in; I saw them all clearly while looking right at Billy, and I never once blinked. I saw the garage, of course, how it was he who made me bring us there. I saw him laughing as Kevin scrawled his drawings across the wall, laughing still when it started to burn. I saw how he made me lie to Madeline and keep on, month after month, learning to be false to my best friend. I heard his awful jokes, whispered in a group. I hated him for all of that—and I hated what he made me see in myself.

I felt like an assassin, trained for this single purpose in life, and poor Billy was my martyr-to-be.

"But listen," I said.

He nodded eagerly.

"You can't tell Kyle."

"Hey, I wouldn't tell him. That'd be like, rubbing it in."

"You can't tell anyone. Because he'll find out, right?"

"Find out?"

"And I don't want to—to hurt him, okay?"

Billy was totally lost.

"I mean," I continued, "I want to be the one to tell him. Myself. You understand."

"Oh, sure."

"It's not fair to Kyle," I said, "if he hears it from you first. I . . . I want to let him down easy."

"Okay," he agreed. "And I respect that, Kerry. I respect you for, you know, for being . . . considerate."

"That's me." I smiled at him.

16

"Microphone?" I looked at Madeline uneasily.

"You know, the little object that lets people hear—"

"I know what a microphone is."

"So where is it?"

I tried to buy time with a deep, long breath. "I'm sure we could *find* one. . . ."

But as I peeked out from one side of the stage and saw the kids filing into the auditorium, I knew it was too—

"It's too *late* to find one," Madeline said. "Weren't you supposed to take care of that ahead of time?"

"Uh-huh," I nodded, and took another peek before I turned back. Madeline shifted her weight and wrung her fingers as if a fuse were burning inside her. Behind her stood our adviser for the assembly, Mr. Hyams. ("He's always good," Ken Doll had said, "for a cause.") But now his perpetual smile was faltering.

Only Marshall, our speaker, didn't seem dismayed that I had forgotten to get the microphone. He had other things to worry about. He was a tall and slender man with short hair and a trim mustache. He dressed in a sweater and corduroys, casual but neat—and he was very, very sick. He might have been a handsome man once; now the skin of his face gripped his cheekbones and the hollows beneath his eyes. Below his left ear, above his collar, and dappled over his left wrist were small purple blotches.

"I'll just sit down for a bit," he said in his hoarse whisper, "before I go on." Mr. Hyams pulled up a folding chair for him.

"Well"—Madeline peered at me—"at least you took care of the lighting crew, right? If they put a spotlight on him and everybody listens, maybe"—together we glanced at Marshall, thinking of his soft, weak voice—"maybe he won't need a mike. . . ."

"Mad," I said, "about the lighting crew . . ."

"*Kerry.*"

"We just never did a final run-through. . . ."

"I put posters all over this school," Madeline all but shouted. "I arranged for the speaker. Just what the hell *did* you do?"

"Girls," Mr. Hyams tried to hush us.

"I did a lot," I said. "There's that table out by the stage . . . with the information. . . ."

Mr. Hyams checked his watch. "It's time to get started."

The three of us glanced out at the crowded auditorium. Ken Doll sat in the front row, tapping his foot and looking around.

"We'll just have to speak . . . loud," Mr. Hyams said, and, leaving us in the wings, strode out to center stage. We heard faint applause and a halfhearted cheer.

Madeline wasn't letting me off. "Did you tell the county commission what kind of information we wanted?"

"Sure," I said. I heard my voice trail off. "I said, uh, AIDS-related . . ."

"So did you look at what they sent over? Statistics! *Diagrams!* They're like pages from a biology textbook. Kids won't read that. Plus there's not a word about prevention. There's not a word about—"

"Sshh, sshh." I gestured out at Mr. Hyams. "He's starting."

Madeline was right, of course. The lighting crew was my responsibility, and I had botched it—just as I had the microphone. I didn't even arrange for a podium to speak from, and now poor Mr. Hyams was out there with his hands in his pockets, ad-libbing it. He'd be lucky if they gave him thirty seconds.

"It's because you were working on that stupid prom," Madeline said.

She was right there, too. I had never known how much work proms were—or how much more fun, too, than calling county agencies and getting put on hold once they realized they were talking to a teenager. "Let's just listen," I said.

Already it was hard to hear Mr. Hyams over the buzz of four hundred separate conversations. "Let's get together and stop this thing," he had to yell to be heard. "We can do it. We have to believe we can do it."

Madeline made a big show of turning her back to me and staring out at the stage.

I edged away for refuge and almost tripped over Marshall. He must have known Madeline and I were arguing, for now and then a tired grin played across his face, as if it amused him what people could waste their energy on.

"He'll introduce you in a second," I said.

"That's fine." He nodded, and smiled slightly.

"You'll have to try"—I felt such a fool, saying it—"to speak loud."

"That's hard," he mouthed, as if he didn't want to squander any strength.

"Don't worry," I assured him. "The kids will listen." But I wasn't so sure.

We heard Mr Hyams say, ". . . a brave young man to share his struggles with you . . . ," and then we saw him looking our way. The kids, for all their inattention, applauded on cue. Marshall stood slowly. I reached forward to help but he was already stepping from the wings to center stage. I rejoined Madeline, a step or two off.

Mr. Hyams retreated to the other side. When the clapping stopped, Marshall stood at the edge of the stage, staring out, as if giving the kids the time to look him over.

"I'm here to tell a story." His first words, hardly more than a whisper, were almost swallowed up by the crowd. "So I need to tell the full story. First, I'm gay. Most of you are not."

Some tittering at that, and I could see Ken Doll squirming in the front row.

"I wish I could say that most of you won't get AIDS, therefore," Marshall continued. "But I can't."

His voice was hoarse. He stopped to clear his throat.

"My friend Paul wasn't gay—but he died of AIDS, anyway. My friend Caroline wasn't gay—and she died, too."

Even from the wings I almost had to hold my breath to hear him.

"When you're standing at someone's coffin—someone who died way too young—you don't really think about whether he's gay, or straight, or even if he knows what he is, because sometimes you can die that young. Children die of AIDS, and babies, too."

Madeline turned to me. "He's better than they deserve." I thought hard how to respond, so I missed his next few words. Then I noticed there wasn't a sound, not from anyone. Only Marshall's pained, halting words. Speaking as loud as he could, his best was only a brave whisper that must have come at some horrible expense to his throat, to his whole body— but the kids were listening. I felt it before I chanced another glance, and then I saw the proof in their postures: leaning forward, their hands to their chins.

"The first time I fell, on the street, I almost didn't want to get up," Marshall was saying. "I thought I would die of embarrassment." He had to take several seconds to clear his throat, and finally he hacked into a handkerchief. I thought how the same act by anybody else would have set the auditorium howling exaggerated groans, cries of gross, *gross*. But no one said a thing. They all waited. I saw a few more change their positions, a few more move to the edges of their seats.

"They're listening," Madeline whispered, her voice full of awe.

"I learned pretty soon," Marshall went on, "that being embarrassed is the least of it."

Though he knew he was sick, he said, he denied it at first. He knew enough of AIDS to recognize some of his symptoms. But he was scared. And cocky. And angry. And another month went by where he didn't see a doctor, and another after that, despite promising himself he would. He didn't change his habits, either—he paused, as if to let that sink in, and when he was sure we understood him, he continued in his thin, weak voice.

I heard Madeline start to sniffle beside me, and I put my arm around her. I couldn't hear every word of Marshall's anymore. I doubted if anyone could. But we heard him, I knew. I started shivering.

"It's okay," Madeline said quietly, and patted my back.

"I'm fighting to save myself now," Marshall said. "That must sound funny. I know how weak I look. But let me tell you something else. I'm fighting to save you, too. Everybody in this room. That's right. A guy who can't walk more than a couple of blocks without having to rest, who has to spend whole days in bed, he thinks he's strong enough to save every person in here." He paused for a breath. "I know I can't do it alone. So help me. Help yourselves. Think about AIDS. Talk about it—to your boyfriend, girlfriend, even your parents. Use condoms. Learn the facts. Don't try to fool yourselves. If you take a good look at me, you'll see the truth."

Marshall thanked them for listening, and was halfway off the stage before the crowd realized he was through. Then they roared. They rose to their feet. Marshall turned once and waved. Madeline and I ran across the stage to thank him, and we both hugged him. I could feel his ribs.

Mr. Hyams led Marshall to the office while the kids emptied out of the auditorium. There wasn't the mad surge for the lunch line you usually saw when an assembly was over. Some remained in their seats, talking. A large group clustered around the AIDS leaflets at the foot of the stage.

"It worked," Madeline said, amazed.

"It was wonderful," I agreed. "He was wonderful."

"I never thought they—"

"I'm sorry about the microphone," I said.

"It doesn't matter." She shrugged, and then hugged me. "It was even better this way." She looked up quickly. "Don't you dare say you knew it all along."

"Okay," I said with a laugh, and we began to climb down the side stairs to the floor of the auditorium. At the bottom of the stairs, by the table full of leaflets, was Kyle—and next to him Billy. I avoided his eyes. I had been so busy lately with the prom it was easy to forget he thought we were going together. Then I saw Linda, Heather, Greg. Even Kevin Montrose. I froze at the sight of them all. "Hey." Madeline bumped into me from behind. "Watch out." But I was sure she hadn't seen them yet, and my first impulse was to retreat, like some film shown backward, up the stairs, into the wings. . . .

"Hey, Ker," Kyle called, reaching up to me.

Madeline stood on the top stair, her face unsure. I saw her mouth start to quiver. We seemed to hold our pose forever.

"That was fantastic," Linda said. She kissed me on the cheek. And then an eternity where we all faced one another and not one of us breathed . . .

Until Linda turned to Madeline as casually as she had to me. "You guys"—she smiled at both of us—"did a great job."

"Awesome," Greg agreed. "We ought to have more stuff

like that." And then everyone spoke at once, "He's right" and "About time" and "That speaker was terrific." There was Madeline, talking earnestly about Marshall to Heather and Linda. I thought I was hallucinating when Kevin Montrose went right up to her and said, "Real good. Real good."

"Thanks," she said, and smiled.

I had been trying to fight back tears ever since Marshall took the stage, and now I just let them come. "Hey, you okay?" Kyle asked. I nodded. I gaped at Madeline and Linda, at Heather, even at Billy, who stood on the edges, at all of them talking together, and I never wanted it to end. As long as they stood together I felt as if I were forgiven. I couldn't wait to get Madeline alone, later, and say, See? They're not so bad, my friends. And Madeline would blush, half-annoyed, half-pleased with me for backing her into a corner from where she could only say, "You're right, Kerry, you're right—"

I felt a sudden tap on my shoulder. Mr. Hyams was at my side, his voice urgent.

"Kerry. Did Mr. Kendall know about Marshall's fee?"

It took me a moment to juggle his words until they made sense.

"His fee . . . oh, right. He asked for two hundred dollars."

"Two hundred and fifty."

"That's it. It's not even for him, it's a donation for the county AIDS hotline."

"But did you clear the fee"—he was as serious as I had ever seen him—"with Mr. Kendall?"

By now Mr. Hyams's tone had alerted everyone. I felt Kyle's arm rest heavy on my shoulder.

"Um—I guess I just . . . I *meant* to. . . ." I looked quickly to Madeline. Like the others, she was waiting for my answer. "I know Mr. Kendall said there was an honorarium."

Mr. Hyams, impatient, finished for me: "He said he made clear the honorarium was fifty."

"Fifty?" Kevin Montrose laughed. "They're paying the guy fifty bucks? You can't even get a keg of beer for fifty bucks."

No one else laughed, though everyone had something to say. "They can't pay him more than fifty bucks?" "Here he comes and gives us this great speech—" "And Kendall's making him *negotiate* in there—"

"You don't remember," Mr. Hyams said to me through the voices, "setting anything definite?"

All I saw were endless columns of prom costs on legal-sized yellow sheets, and how easy it was to forget what seemed like little details.

"Kerry?" Mr. Hyams waited.

"It's my fault," I said. "I never got back to Mr. Kendall. It's my fault." Mr. Hyams was already hurrying back to the office.

"Kendall's such a jerk," Heather moaned.

"He gets a standing ovation," Kyle said, "and they treat him like that."

More agreement, more outrage, and then Billy said, "I can't believe it. The guy comes all the way over here—"

My eyes settled on Madeline, shoulder to shoulder with Heather.

"—just so Kendall," Billy continued, "can Jew him out of a couple hundred bucks."

I heard it right away. So did Madeline, for I saw her whole expression cave in at the slur. First there was shock—her shoulders slumped a little—and then a look I recognized well. Her face contracted into a miserable kind of I-told-you-so come true. Though we were all standing together, she seemed apart again, by several feet.

I thought everyone would jump on him for that, so I only said, *"Billy,"* sternly, as if I might shame him, but everyone was going on, abusing Kendall, complaining, and nobody heard me. Most of them, I realized, hadn't found a thing offensive in his words. By then Madeline had slipped away, up the aisle of the auditorium and into the darkness under the balcony, and no one seemed to notice. I watched her, over Kyle's shoulder, hoping with every step she would come back to us.

Then Kevin said, "Hey, it's lunch, remember," and Heather teased back, "Oh, right, your feeding time," and I might have dreamed the whole last minute, and what Billy said, the way everybody broke away so easily from the stage.

Kyle lingered, holding my arm. When the others had gone ahead he kissed me. "I'm really proud of you," he said. "This was great."

I tried to smile, and gestured to the leaflets. "Did you get a chance to look at any of these?"

"Yeah." He went over and scooped up a few. "Well, not yet."

"They're good," I said. "They're important."

"They are," he agreed. "I'm going to read through them."

Then Greg called us from the door of the auditorium. He was driving, if we wanted to go out for lunch. We hurried up the aisle after him, and just once, at the door, I looked back at where Marshall had stood, and to the wings where Madeline and I had listened, rubbing our eyes to keep back the tears.

There, on the edge of the stage, I saw the pile of leaflets where Kyle had laid them.

17

"You're going to wear *that*?" my mother said.

Her face slowly grew darker, like a cloud throwing a hillside into shadow. Half her lips seemed to disappear in a strained pucker. She craned her neck forward to peer at some part of me, then fell back against the sofa.

"You're wearing that," she repeated, "to the prom?"

I didn't even want to show her the dress Dad had bought for me. But when I struggled in the front door on Sunday she was all wrapped up on one side of the broken couch, staring straight at the bulky package in my arms.

I hadn't even thought about buying one yet, but as soon as I mentioned the prom, Dad sounded shocked.

"Kerry, you don't have your *dress* yet?"

"It's barely April," I told him. "The prom's a month away."

"So what are we waiting for?" he teased. "Let's get you something that lets you strut your stuff." Of course he didn't say anything about being comfortable. In the dress my hips felt so snug I couldn't help but walk with an exaggerated roll, as if I were showing off my butt. The neckline was low, and snuggled my breasts together so it was a little tricky taking normal breaths, but I knew aerobics wasn't exactly the point here. Black and white ruffles covered my shoulders.

Faint vertical striping emphasized every contour of my shape. Just above my knees there was a little frill of black lace. But when I emerged from the dressing room at the store and gazed in the three-way mirror, I felt—striking, so slim and sultry.

Even though I was enjoying all the planning, it was the first time the prom had seemed really special, and I probably didn't get more than one whole minute of feeling that way before I thought of Billy. Not Kyle, no, not my boyfriend, but Billy! The closer the prom, the more I wondered what I had been thinking of when I said yes to him. I had to tell him the truth. It wouldn't be easy, but—

Then I pictured the lighter, that nearly naked girl with her mindless smile, and for a moment I was livid. I let the anger flare. He deserved it, I told myself.

"Kerry."

He deserved it.

"Come on, stand up straight. Let me see you."

When I looked up at the mirror I met my dad's admiring glance, and Billy was forgotten. Dad just shook his head, and blushed, and said, "My goodness. Kerry. My oh my . . ."

Over the weekend, modeling the dress for him, I had felt like a cover girl.

In front of my mother I felt like a whore.

"Isn't that outfit a little . . . *bold*?" she suggested.

I avoided her eyes. "It's supposed to be."

"Well, it was nice of your father to pay for it," she finally said. "Did he write a check?"

"You don't like it, do you?"

"There's *something*"—she resettled her position on the sofa—"something of the alley cat in that outfit."

I paused while the words sank in. In about two seconds I swooped from embarrassment to anger.

"Dad said I look like a real fox."

"Your father and I"—she sighed—"have different views of the animal kingdom."

I stormed to my room—and it wasn't easy, either, in that tight dress—slammed my door, and then I listened: no footsteps, no reaction. Fine. Let her sit on that sofa forever. She was jealous of my whole life, that was it, and she had nobody but herself to blame.

There on my desk, propped up against a lamp, was a letter from Ridley College.

I pounced on it, and like a maniac I ripped open the envelope so fiercely that half the letterhead came off in my hand.

> Dear Kerry Dunbar:
>   Congratulations! The Dean of Admissions at Ridley College is pleased to admit you to the freshman class. . . .

The words grew watery before my eyes. Was I crying, or faint? I blinked and jumped ahead.

> I'm sure you're well aware how competitive the selection process is at a school like Ridley, and therefore you should be proud for . . .

I was trembling and needed to pee, but I intended to finish the letter if I wet my pants doing it.

> Soon you'll receive your catalog of fall courses

Bells clanged, fireworks exploded in my brain. You're in! a voice shrieked. You made it! cried another; I heard loud, delirious voices—

as well as all decisions regarding your applications for financial aid and housing. . . .

—the voices of Heather, of Linda and Kyle, Miss Tufts and my dad—

But not my mother's.

The victory dance my feet had been performing came to a sudden stop.

She hadn't even told me the letter was here. She knew how long I'd been waiting. It was as if she had kept me downstairs, arguing over the dress, on purpose. And why not, after all? It was just another gloomy, boring day for her. So what if her daughter's future sat sealed on her desk upstairs.

I hated her then, for being so selfish.

I couldn't even go down and hug her.

The hugs would have to wait till Monday, from the people who really cared about me.

I read the letter again, then another time. Maybe I would make some calls that night, just a few, so I could hear myself say it: Guess what? I got into Ridley. I could start with Rhonda.

There was a phone in my mother's room, and before I called anyone I ran through the messages on the answering machine. They were all for me, as usual, Linda calling just to gossip, Paula from the Prom Committee agitating over a detail. Then a man's voice came on, deep and weary, and I knew this message wasn't mine.

"Hello, Martha? This is David. I, uh, I have some bad news for you. I should probably just let you hear it for yourself on Monday, but I wanted to prepare you. Anyway . . . they're not going to do your project. I heard it from a friend on the county board. I asked if this is just a deferral, and he said he didn't think so. It's the budget, you know, plus there's a thought that too much attention to teen pregnancies might be, get this, controversial. Can you believe it? I said is it better to ignore the problem? But really, it's not my friend's fault, and—"

The voice beeped off abruptly, and I could hear Heather's bubbly tone asking me if I wanted to go shopping, and if I did, to call her back. . . .

I turned off the machine and sat in my mother's dimly lit bedroom. I should go to her, I thought. I had to. So what if I was angry. Just tell her how sorry I was at the news.

At the top of the stairs I heard the old springs on the sofa as she changed her position, and the sound alone made me hold back.

I saw myself saying, I heard the message. I feel so bad for you. And hugging her, sitting beside her—

But I remembered the broken frame of the sofa, where two people couldn't sit together if they wanted to.

I tried to imagine more, but nothing came. Not her hugging me back, not her saying, It's all right, or even It hurts like hell, and certainly not her expression softening for one instant. Nothing like the hint of tears.

In the morning, I decided. I backed off from the staircase. Sure. Maybe she'd even bring it up by then. If not, I would, certainly.

I shut the door to my room, read the letter from Ridley once again, and stood for a long time in front of my closet, marveling at the sleek tapered lines of my new dress.

Part Four

A PROM LIKE YOU
NEVER IMAGINED

18

On the cloud of Ridley I floated down the halls, from one "Congratulations" to the next. Kyle cheered, Linda and Heather squealed as if we were in middle school. Miss Tufts almost danced for joy, and raced to her bulletin board with a gold pin. I could almost feel the buzz of the news through the school. Kerry Dunbar, Ridley College, they were saying, buzz buzz buzz. . . .

That almost made up for the evenings I lay on the bed in my mother's room and stared at her phone, yearning to call Madeline, and afraid to. I'd circle in on the phone the way you approach an unsuspecting animal, swallow, almost tap out her number, and then draw back. She didn't even know about Ridley yet, and how could I tell her? It was hard enough to look at her after the AIDS assembly. Every time I saw her I saw her as she was that day, after Billy's slur, slinking off, as if she were the one who had done something wrong.

At night, in my bed, I heard Billy's voice—*Jew him out of a couple hundred bucks*. I saw the crude cartoon Kevin had drawn inside her garage. Of course that was wrong, that was stupid, I was never a part of that, I defended myself. But you couldn't just ignore things like that and turn your back. It was the words themselves that lingered, like some stinking odor you couldn't get away from.

I stood and stared at the name next to mine.

Teddy Mattson.

Right there, on Mrs. McGann's bulletin board in English: Special Author Project.

Teams:

Kerry Dunbar. I blinked hard, but it was still there. Teddy Mattson.

"I know you'd rather choose the person you work with." Mrs. McGann stood at the front of the room, clasping her hands, beaming out her joy of life and English. "But you'd probably just pick someone *comfortable,* someone who agrees with everything you say or do. This is much more of a challenge."

But working with Teddy Mattson wasn't a challenge, it was a sentence. Life without parole.

After class I went up to Mrs. McGann to make my appeal.

"Maybe someone was absent today and that person could be my partner," I said, "because, you know, Teddy is, well . . ."

She had beautiful blue eyes—hard to believe, with all that poetry she read—but they fixed me now without compassion. "I thought it might be good for you—and for your grades, which seem to have plummeted since the first quarter—to work with a really creative, innovative A student."

I swallowed, with difficulty. "Teddy Mattson is an A student?"

"Oh, yes."

"He never even has a pen."

"Well, that's true. But he writes some fine papers—they're a little, oh, strange, sometimes—"

"I'll bet."

"But very original."

"Do you know what it's going to be like, working with Teddy Mattson?"

"You'll need patience."

"I'll need a *translator*." Okay, I was ready to beg. "Mrs. McGann, can't you just let me work with someone else? Can't you"—I saw her across the room and jumped on the thought—"can't you get me together with Madeline?"

"Kerry, that's just what I mean," she said with a laugh. "If I let you, you'd all just choose your—"

"No, no, we're not that close, Madeline and I. You don't understand, we're really nothing alike."

"Nonsense. You're the best of friends."

"Yeah." I sighed, and glanced at Madeline. "That's us." I turned back to Mrs. McGann. "Can you at least tell me who our author is?"

She sat back in her chair. "You know I said I'd announce that in class tomorrow."

"You matched me with Teddy Mattson," I complained. "Haven't I had enough surprises?"

Nervously I unfolded the piece of paper and read the name. *"Thomas Hardy,"* I whined, and threw back my head in despair.

"Wow, Thomas Hardy, cool," Teddy Mattson said. "We got lucky."

I glared at him. "Nothing about this project has been lucky." The room was filled with gasps and moans as other groups discovered their authors. "He's old, he's dead, he's English," I said. "His books are seven thousand pages long and there's hardly any dialogue."

He wasn't that bad, I thought, really. Earlier this year we had read *Tess of the D'Urbervilles,* which was okay—but long—about a girl who got pregnant and how it ruined her life. I had even mentioned it to my mom, since she worked so much with teenage pregnancies. She knew all about the book, of course. It was her favorite book, she said (which was really depressing, to find you didn't even know your mother's favorite book).

No, what was worse than Thomas Hardy was Teddy Mattson. All week long he had been making a mockery of Pride Week. On Clash Day he wore a plain black suit. He clashed later, on Blue-and-White Day, in a plaid sport jacket, striped seventies bell-bottoms, and a paisley tie. Friday was the Sports Awards Assembly, when the best athletes in the school were called up on stage to receive plaques (Kyle's, of course, one of the biggest). At one point, after a big cheer for the football team, a large and homely cheerleader with hair like a mophead darted from the wings, kicked her hairy legs and led a mock cheer, and disappeared out the other side before an enraged Ken Doll or any of the jocks could catch her. It was Teddy, the whole school knew it, but like a seasoned bank robber he had disposed of the outfit by the time anyone found him, calmly reading *Sports Illustrated* in the back of the library. "I've been here all the time," he claimed, and not one of the library aides could say he hadn't.

That was my partner.

Mrs. McGann wasn't going to let us work in class, either, with the AP exams in just a few weeks, so we had to make arrangements to meet somewhere else.

"We'll have to get busy," I said. "We've only got three weeks till this is due."

Teddy looked unconcerned. "Well, time's an illusion, I always say. No need to panic."

Time's an illusion? Around the room *normal* people in pairs were already writing things down. "We'll never get this done!" I yelled at him.

Teddy's pale green eyes glistened like the surface of the moon through a telescope. "I've already got my part done."

Maybe I could signal to Mrs. McGann for help.

"But if you want to rehearse a little more—"

"*More?*"

"—maybe we should meet this week. How about tomorrow at lunch?"

"I can't," I said defensively. "I've got a prom meeting."

"*Ooohhh,*" Teddy said. "We can't miss that."

"I can't," I snapped back. "I'm in charge."

"Ahh, so I'm working with the prom queen—"

"There is no prom queen." I took out a piece of paper and stared down at it. "Let's meet next Monday night."

"I can't," he said. "I have a flying saucer convention—"

"Teddy!"

"Okay, Monday night it is. Where do we meet?"

In a padded cell, I thought. With plenty of attendants.

"My house is pretty messy," Teddy said. "My brother and I, we started this dust ball collection. . . ."

"We can't meet at my house," I said decisively.

Something in my tone jarred him out of his looniness, if only for a moment. "Okay," he said. "How about the library?"

Neutral ground! I seized it. "Fine. The library it is. Seven o'clock."

"Okay, Prom Queen."

"Don't call me that."

"Right. But"—he stared at me curiously—"who are you then, anyway?"

I managed to put off the meeting with Teddy Mattson for another week. And in that extra week, since I sure didn't have time to plow through Thomas Hardy and his five-hundred-page novels, I bought three or four of the Cliffs Notes for his books, and read those instead. Secretly, of course. I would die if anyone knew. Me, Kerry Dunbar, onetime valedictorian wannabe, skimming plot summaries like some desperate C student.

154 / Scott Johnson

Except I remembered that, at least for the second half of the year, I *was* a C student.

The following Monday evening at seven o'clock I stood in the library, scanning the desks. Of course he'd be late. I scowled.

Then I noticed an older man with sunglasses staring at me. I tried to ignore him, but soon he was grimacing strangely and motioning me over. I was just about to complain about him to the front desk when he sputtered, "Hey, Prom Queen," in a loud Donald Duck voice that made everybody turn.

"Sorry, Teddy," I said curtly. "I can't understand why I didn't recognize you." He was wearing an old-fashioned green tweed suit, complete with vest, the kind with three buttons on the front, skinny little lapels, and cuffs on the pants. He must have got the suit in a Goodwill store. His blond hair was knotted up in a little ponytail and his wire-frame glasses would have made him look intellectual, if I didn't already know he was just insane.

"You're late," he chided me.

"I thought time was an illusion," I grumbled. And then, up close, I saw his face. "Teddy," I gasped, as I took it all in. First his bottom lip, puffed to twice its normal size, and an ugly half-inch sore in the corner. His cheeks were a bright, raw red, and along his jaw a cut had turned black with drying, scabby skin.

"That's nothing," he said. "Look." He lifted up his sunglasses, trying to make a joke of it, blinking rapidly like a cartoon character. Deep black bruises shadowed his eyes. The hair of his left eyebrow was clumped and matted.

"What happened?"

"Oh, uh"—he readjusted his sunglasses—"just some of the guys on the football team stopped by to let me know how much they liked my sense of humor. You know, Kevin Montrose, and Greg Del Sandro—"

"And Billy?" I leaned across the table. "Billy Stockton?"

He paused to remember. "No, I don't think Billy was there. I distinctly heard only two voices grunting."

"But why? Because of that stunt you pulled at the assembly?"

"I guess so. I'd be hurt if it was just *me* they didn't like."

"You have to call the police," I said.

"Oh, come on."

"You have to. Somebody," I insisted, "has to be brave enough to stand up . . ."

He looked confused. "Stand up for what?"

"Nothing." I shook my head. "Didn't your parents want to call the police?"

"Sure." He shrugged. "I talked them out of it. I told them I had it coming. For being such a smartass." Teddy laughed. "My dad's been waiting eighteen years for me to say that. Think he was going to ruin it by calling the police?"

I tried to sound as dispassionate as I could. "But Billy Stockton wasn't there?"

"Nope," Teddy said. "I guess I'm just a two-jock job."

We finally got to Thomas Hardy. It wasn't easy. Once in a while Teddy would grimace and grab his side, or touch his face without thinking first, and we'd both cringe. He let me talk for a while. He let me suggest how I thought we should divide up the presentation and each work on our separate parts. I would give plot summaries of the various novels, and Teddy could do the biographical part. He watched me, his green eyes glassy as if he were hypnotized. Then I reached into my notebook and he spied the bright yellow and black of—

"Cliffs Notes!" he shouted, loud enough for dead librarians the world over to shiver in their graves.

"Cliffs Notes," he said again, rising, despite the pain, and pointing, and making a noise like a fire alarm.

"Teddy," I pleaded. "I only—"

The librarian was staring our way, and Teddy sat down quickly.

"I only glanced through them," I said defensively, "to get some ideas. Of course I'm going to read the—"

"What's wrong with Cliffs Notes?" he asked innocently.

"What do you mean?"

"What do *you* mean?" he said. "You act like you got caught doing something naughty."

"Wait a minute, you *stand* there and *point* at me—"

"Because the minute I mentioned them your face got red. What's the big deal? You think you're the only person in the world using Cliffs Notes?"

"Look, I've got this prom to plan for, and I'm sorry if I have a social life, but I have better things to do than sit around reading novels—"

"Okay, great. Read Cliffs Notes. But don't be so concerned about what other people think."

"I'm not," I said.

He only smiled at me. He had a decent smile, really; I could tell through the bruises.

I tried to get us back on track. "What do you think of my idea? For the project?"

His head fell onto the desk and he began to snore.

"Teddy."

He snored louder. The librarian was stalking back and forth behind the microfiche viewer.

He looked up. "It's *boring*. It's okay, it's like most of what passes for education, but let's not pretend it's not boring."

"I'm sorry," I snapped. "I guess I'm boring, too. You can't help the kind of person you are."

"Can't you?"

"What about you? Is that why you act so crazy? To be somebody you're not?"

Now Teddy looked hurt. "Crazy?" he whined. "Me?" And then he grinned, and I did, too. "So go on with your idea," he said. "I need the sleep."

I referred to novels and the characters in them, but he corrected me on so many points I finally got fed up and said, "All right, all right, I'll read the stupid books," and he said, "No, no, don't put yourself out on my account," and I said, "No, really, I insist," and he said, "Promise?" So I did, and I felt tricked, and I knew that was his scheme all along. We must have gotten loud, for by the time I was ready to leave and had checked out a couple of Hardy's books (ten pounds, the two of them) the librarian was sighing pointedly and examined my card as if it were a passport.

"Teddy," I asked. "Is it true you got into Cornell?"

"I swear to God." He raised his hand as in an oath. "And you"—he pointed accusingly—"got into Ridley."

"Are you excited about college?" I asked. What I really wanted to talk about was how I was excited.

"I guess so." He thumbed through a Hardy. "If I go."

"If you go? Are you kidding?"

"Ehh. I'm looking into some other things."

"Other schools? What could be better than—"

"Other things. Like, maybe, not going right on to school. I think I'm going to build trails."

"What?"

"In the Olympic Mountains. In Washington State. I won't get paid much, but I'll get room and board, and I'll build trails with the National Park Service, you know, clear brush, repair footbridges, and I get to watch eagles and bighorn sheep on my lunch hour. It's like a scholarship, really, except I'll get my hands dirty."

"I don't know," I said as we walked out. "A lot of kids would die to get into—"

"Hey, you need a ride?" Teddy asked abruptly, and led me to his car, a dented, bumper-stickered Volkswagen Beetle. Most of it was red. The top was yellow and the left rear bumper blue. The car had to be older than we were.

"Cool, huh?" he raved. "I bought it from a real, genuine ex-hippie. And look." He led me to the passenger side. "An authentic flower decal." He opened the door for me. In the dark, in his tweed suit, he could have been a chauffeur. "I'll bet this car was at Woodstock," he said. We waited while the engine revved itself up, like a rickety old fan. "Or maybe San Francisco."

"Why not both?" I smiled.

"Yeah," he agreed, enthused. "That's right! Why not?" I laughed until he removed his sunglasses and the last light of day highlighted his tender, swollen face.

So I had a lot of Thomas Hardy to read, and in a hurry, too, with our presentation coming up in ten days, and the prom right after it. I retreated to the auditorium and found a dark corner and tried to read big chunks of *Far from the Madding Crowd*. Teddy said it was "hot." It was good, anyway, but what it was best at was keeping me occupied for twenty or thirty pages at a time, and keeping everything else shut out. I'd check my watch and see a half hour had passed, and realize it was one of the few half hours in the last four months where I hadn't thought of Madeline, or the fire, or the lighter tucked away in Ms. Trice's basement room. Good old Thomas Hardy to the rescue. His characters' lives were just about as screwed up as mine was.

Only once was I interrupted. By Billy, of course. He seated himself facing backward in the row ahead of me and peered down at the title, mouthing it to himself.

"I hope," I said without looking up from the page, "you're here to talk about the prom."

"Uh . . ."

"The prom, and nothing else."

"Yeah. Sure, the prom . . ."

"Because I don't want to hear about anything else. Right?"

"Okay."

I tucked Thomas Hardy into my purse and readied myself.

"I was wondering, when someone says, 'Billy, who you taking to the prom?' I'm, like, I don't know what to say. You said you didn't want me to—"

"Say you're taking a mystery woman. Okay?"

"A mystery woman." He looked intrigued.

"A mystery woman no one's ever seen before."

"That sounds good, I guess."

"Just trust me," I said sweetly. "That's the best way to work it." I dug out the Hardy book again, as if Billy might start taking hints.

"So you haven't told him."

I glanced over the top of the page. "What about it?"

"Well, if I was going to break up with someone, I'd want to get it over with."

"I think I know what's best," I said.

I stared at him in the dim auditorium light. Not a sound reached us from the halls.

"Billy," I said. "What do you know about Teddy Mattson getting beat up?"

He wiggled restlessly. "That stupid Kevin—"

"Were you there?"

"Uh-uh."

"Tell me the truth."

"I told Kevin he didn't deserve it. He's a jerk, sure, but—"

"Oh, so you knew about it."

"Kevin wanted me in on it. I told him no. I told him it was stupid."

"But you sat by and let it happen when you knew—"

"No! I thought I talked him out of it. 'Yeah, you're right, let's forget it,' Kevin told me. And that was the last I heard of it, till I saw the guy's face the other day."

I stared down at my hands.

"Kerry," Billy asked. "Do you remember . . . that detective?"

"Of course I do," I snapped. "What about him?"

"I was thinking . . . if I was going to—"

The book slipped from my fingers to the floor. I reached down for the book and when I had control of my face I sat up again. "You're back to that, now."

"I can't help it. I thought, maybe, with time, I'd get over it—"

"Get over it!" Suddenly I was sneering at him. "Their garage burns down, Madeline loses a scholarship, your buddy Kevin writes that stuff all over the walls, and you want to *get over it.*"

"That's what I mean. I can't. It's always in my head—"

"It's always in my head, too. How long do you think I want to carry that fire around with me?"

His eyes grew big, as if it were finally the reaction he'd been waiting for. "You see?"

"But I'm doing it," I bullied him, "aren't I? And that's what you have to do. You just have to carry it around with you." I heard the words as if someone were speaking them for me.

He rubbed his brow, and I knew it was just a way to avoid my eyes. "I'm not sure that I can."

"And now you're going to run to a detective."

"I didn't *say* I would."

"So good. Fine. Confess. You caused it, after all. You and Kevin."

"I know."

I expected anything then, except "I know."

"Kerry"—he leaned in close—"I'm still scared. Okay?" I tried to keep still, but I found myself nodding. He looked so miserable. "I feel so goddamn *guilty.* Day after day." He drew a breath. "Can you understand that?"

Now I was the one looking away.

"They would have caught you by now," I assured him. "I think you got away with it."

"Great," he said sourly. "I feel so much better."

The bell rang to end the period, and through the auditorium doors we could hear the first voices as classes changed. Soon the random noises grew into an avalanche of sound that made the auditorium no place for talk like this.

"Billy." I should have been leaving, too, for my next class, but I held on. "Why do you tell all those stupid jokes? Those racist jokes. Those Jewish jokes."

He squinted, as if trying to spot a receiver in some distant end zone. "I don't know. I never thought *why*," he said.

"Well, do. Try it. Tell me why."

"I guess"—he looked confused, until he fell upon an answer—"I guess 'cause you *laugh,* Kerry," he said. "You and everybody else."

19

"Jack Dunbar, homefinder."

"Dad."

"Kerry."

"Dad. Can you hear me?" My dad insisted on using his car phone, even though it hissed and crackled whenever he hit a pothole. This time there was a metallic *snap-snap-snap,* and an occasional *ka-boom* as if he were banging the phone against a drum set. "There's all sorts of static on the line."

"That's funny, I can hear you fine."

"Dad, you know, about Ridley—"

"I am so proud of my daughter, did I tell you that?"

"I know. Do you remember I told you about that financial aid application I made?"

"Sure do."

"And those scholarship applications?"

"You're not giving me more good news, are you?"

"Uh . . . no, I'm not. They turned me down on the finan- cial aid."

Silence. More *ka-booms.*

"Dad?"

"They turned you down for *everything*?"

"Everything. They said I didn't qualify." I shut my eyes

and rested my head against the kitchen wall, waiting. "Mom said I should call you and make sure you knew."

"Well, honey . . . so what?"

"So what?"

"If they're not going to give you any money, who cares? We're still going to Ridley, right?"

"I—"

"We are, aren't we?"

"Sure," I said. "We are."

"Damn the expense. Full speed ahead." There were times when I needed a guy like my dad, when his enthusiasm zapped through the phone like high voltage. Putting the money together? Not a problem, he bubbled, if you were creative about it. He rambled on about second mortgages and insurance policies and tax shelters, and how getting *into* a school like Ridley was the hard part, *paying* for it was only a challenge, and "You know I love a challenge, right, Kerry?"

"Well . . . sure." Already I could feel myself standing taller. "Right."

"I am so proud," he said. "Wait till you see the car. I've got a great big Ridley decal on the rear window. Almost blocks out my whole rearview mirror."

"But Dad, couldn't that cause an accident?"

"Hey," he said. "Who's looking back?"

For every step Kyle took there was another kid reaching over to pat his shoulder, shake his hand, gesture thumbs-up, holler out his name. Two days earlier he had made his decision: Layton College, in North Carolina. ("A hoops powerhouse," he had told me. "Connections everywhere!") He was getting a full scholarship ("A single in the jock dorm," he raved) and summer work opportunities. ("Summer work," he said with a laugh, "is the code for when the alumni pay for my stereo and loan me a car!") I stood at the end of the hall and watched him fight his way through the crowd, to me. Still a couple of worshipers away, he reached out, over them, cupped the back of my head, and kissed me hard.

"Hey, I've got the Beamer today. Let's cut last period and go for a ride. I want to show you something."

What he wanted to show me was his tux. He took me to a formal wear shop, paraded me right past a little salesman to show me the complete outfit he had reserved. After that we drove to a chauffeur service, where he led me past the long, sleek limousines, poised and powerful as sharks, and let me pick our color.

I should have been excited, I supposed, with the prom just a week away, but I wasn't. I was weary, and irritable—and more and more I was scared. It was okay, a month ago, to tell myself I could cut Billy's heart out on prom night and just walk away. It was different now. Real. Somehow the Billy in the auditorium deserved less of my rage. And though I could imagine his shock when my mother would tell him, She left a half hour ago with Kyle, that still seemed the easiest way out—easier than telling him the truth. Now that he was talking again of turning himself in, who could tell what direction he'd shoot off to when he found out I'd used him so. Why shouldn't he run to that detective in a blind rage and name all of us, or maybe just name me?

And here was Kyle, humming happily along with the radio. I readjusted myself to watch him behind the wheel. "You know what gets me?" My voice was pure resentment. "You stroll past all those fancy tuxes and limos, and you don't even give them a second thought."

"Yeah?" He sounded pleased. "Does it look that way?"

"And come to think of it, you never even *asked* me to the prom."

"Hey—I knew who you were going with." He grinned, and it only faded a little when he looked at me. "Come on, relax."

"Even getting a full scholarship at Layton. The way you act about it, so cool—"

"Yeah?" He was loving this.

"It's as if you don't care."

Only then did I hear a hint of annoyance. "Of course I care." He threw me a curious glance as he deftly passed the car ahead of us. "Sometimes," he said, peering ahead, "I wonder if you know me at all."

"Oh, but I do," I said.

"For instance . . ."

"For instance, I knew it would never once occur to you how far it is from North Carolina to Pennsylvania."

"Why?" he wondered. "What's in Pennsylvania?"

"Ridley," I said.

He stared ahead. I hurried on.

"The first night you told me about Layton, I went home and looked it up in the atlas. Would you do something like that?"

"Kerry . . ."

"You wouldn't. Because it hardly even matters to you that Layton is eight hundred forty-seven miles from Ridley."

"So what are you saying?"

I didn't know, exactly. I sure didn't plan this. All I knew was what brought me to it, too much of *tuxes* and *limos* and *jock dorms*, and Billy, as stable as a defective firecracker, lurking in the background.

"I guess I'm saying, if you love me, you sure don't show it."

As soon as I said *love*, I knew I had made a mistake. My stomach tightened. I girded myself for some onslaught from Kyle—but nothing came. He was quiet for several seconds, concentrating on the road. I was ready to offer up, I'm sorry. I shouldn't have said that. But he spoke first—or tried to. The words came in brief spurts, as if he had to wind himself up. He stammered, sighed a few times, frustrated, started again, and went silent. He pursed his lips and squinted a bit, and I saw a different Kyle now, someone just a little unsure. It felt strange, but I liked it. I wouldn't have helped him out of this for the world.

"Why are we talking like this?" he managed at last. "*Love. College. Right now, what does it matter?*"

"Maybe it doesn't," I said, and made sure I turned away. "And maybe it does."

But by the time I turned back to him, everything had changed. The Kyle who stumbled with his words, who seemed jittery when I even touched the surface of all I had to say—was gone. The Kyle I was so accustomed to tapped in a CD and squeezed my leg, all in one effortless motion. I wondered how to get the other one back. I blinked hard, but I knew it was too late.

Prom night. He had quite a program, too, as complicated and to the minute as I had scheduled the prom itself. I would have to be ready by seven, he told me. We'd arrive exactly at eight, with Linda, Heather, Greg, Kevin, Billy—

"Billy?" I asked without thinking.

"Yeah. Hey, did you hear who he's going with?"

"I have no idea," I said quickly.

"Called her a *mystery woman,*" Kyle snorted. "What a dork. She's probably some eighth-grader."

"So after the prom," I said, "then what?"

"Then"—he smiled, and his hand massaged my leg—"it'll be time for some *serious* partying."

I was tired just thinking about it. "Where could we go at that hour?"

"That's just it. We need somebody's house. Where there won't be parents around."

"My mother"—I stirred uneasily—"is always home."

"Yeah, but, what about that old lady next door to you? With the basement?"

"You mean Ms. Trice?"

"Yeah. She's the deaf one, right?"

"She's not really deaf—"

"But she can hardly hear. And you said she never locks her doors."

"Kyle, no."

"It's *perfect*. We can stay there till morning, and she won't even hear us."

"No. I refuse. Not Ms. Trice's."

"Oh, right, it's okay for you to break in when your party gets out of control—"

"That wasn't breaking in. And this is different."

"Why?"

"Because it—" Well, why? Because it was *my* special room? Because loading it up with a bunch of drunk friends would rub out the last of my memories left in it? Because there was something tucked away in one of the cupboards that I didn't want anybody near?

How stupid would that sound?

Stupid to this Kyle, anyway. I thought longingly of that other boy, beside me just a few minutes ago, and how much I had to tell him.

"It's private," Kyle went on. "We can put an ice chest in beforehand, maybe even a keg. And"—he turned to me, his voice growing husky—"you said there was even a couch or two. . . ."

"I don't want to," I said. We stopped at a light. "Don't tell everybody about this. Don't tell *anybody*."

"Why not?" he smiled slyly, putting his arm around me. "Because then you won't be able to turn them down?"

"That's right," I said, looking away.

He drew me to him and kissed me, and he seemed to know exactly when the light turned green to let me go.

"I already told them," he said.

The list of activities in the yearbook under Paula Gamble's name was always three inches long, and from the beginning of the prom preparations she had kept me busy with phone calls to make, caterers to interview, deejays and bands to audition, florists to contact, parents to soothe. Now I watched from the wings as, center stage, she talked about the prom to the entire senior class. "You ought to come out there with me," she had urged. "Stand in the spotlight. Feel some *excitement*."

"I've had my share, thanks."

All I could think of while Paula spoke to the kids was how that morning, in English, a note had flipped onto my desk. I unfolded it in my lap, certain it was from Linda, or maybe even Teddy. It wasn't. I tried not to gape when I recognized Madeline's handwriting.

I need to talk to you, she had written. It's urgent.

She knows.

I heard a wheezing, realized it was mine, and forced myself to look up and follow Mrs. McGann as she wrote notes on the board. The chalk lines must have formed words, but nothing I could make sense of.

They must have found something new, new evidence. Or somebody told. Or they ran through our stories for the hundredth time and snagged the one that just didn't check out. . . .

I thought to try and peek at Madeline, maybe grin or nod to buy some time, but a fear of the judgment on her face kept me staring straight ahead.

When the door at the back of the room suddenly opened, I must have jumped. Mrs. McGann and the entire class—except me—turned to see Paula duck her head in. "Mr. Kendall needs Kerry Dunbar for the prom assembly," she said.

Mrs. McGann glanced curiously down at me. "I forgot," I said hoarsely. "I forgot, Mrs. McGann, to tell you, I'm sor—"

"Go, go." She fluttered her hands good-naturedly. "The prom conquers all. How can literature compete?"

I gathered my books, trying to still my shaking hands, and when I passed Madeline I paused by her desk. Then one of my books started to slip, and as I jerked to catch it I bumped the shoulder of the girl sitting next to me. "Sorry," I whispered to her, and finally dared to raise my eyes to Madeline—

"Kerry, Come *on*," Paula nagged from the door.

It was all the excuse I needed to get away.

Now while Paula strolled with the microphone as if she were the star of her own talk show, chirping to the seniors about parking rules, I lingered in the shadows offstage.

It's better that Madeline knows, I nodded to myself, the way demented people on the street agree with the voices in their heads.

I could never have told her. It's better she confront me.

". . . somebody you have a lot to be grateful to." Paula's words reached me in unconnected fragments.

". . . to take some questions with me, Kerry Dunbar."

My head snapped up. Paula was gesturing for me to come out there. I tried to shake my head no, but the kids were cheering along for fun, and it was clear Paula wasn't going on until I joined her.

I couldn't have been more dazed. Paula had me tell them all about the menu—I probably left out the entrée in my world record pace to finish and get off—but she held on to my arm as she asked the kids for questions. Luckily she answered most of them, but when somebody whined how the tickets were too high, Paula tossed that one to me. "Well, Kerry?"

"You'll see," I tried to reassure them. "It'll be worth it. It'll be a prom like . . . like . . ."

Paula blared over my shoulder. "A prom," she promised, as her voice broke and she squeaked, "like you never imagined." And at that the senior class erupted in a loud roar. Paula threw up her fist in triumph, and they cheered some more, until finally Ken Doll came out to wave it down.

"That was *excellent*." Paula hugged me. The kids were booing as Ken Doll shooed them off to their next class. "We *own* this school right now."

I nodded, kneeling down to wrap up the microphone cord.

When I looked up, Madeline stood a few feet away from me, as casually as if she were waiting for a bus.

"You were good," Madeline said. I mumbled thanks.

"I got your note," I began. "I couldn't answer. Mrs. McGann was watching, you know—"

"That's okay."

My eyes went everywhere, picking out escape routes. *Better* that she confront me? What was I thinking of?

She glanced up, overhead. "I never knew how hot it was, here on stage."

"It's the lights," I said. We stood, still circled in the almost white pool of the spotlight. I could feel myself perspiring.

"Mad," I nearly choked. "What is it?"

She was stalling. And then I saw how long I'd been waiting for this moment, wanting it, all along. Yes, it was better, no matter what happened afterward. . . .

"Go on." I swallowed. "Say it."

"Well—Kerry, is it too late . . ."

"It's *not* too late. You hear me? It's *not.*"

"It's not too late to get prom tickets?"

"Prom tickets?" I added up the words, and then again. "You want . . . prom tickets?"

"For me"—she fidgeted—"and for Andrew. Is it too late?"

I should have felt safe. Rescued once again. I should have sighed in relief that it was clear she knew nothing and I would never be caught, and I could just ease out from under the weight I'd been lugging.

Instead, I was crushed. For that was how Madeline saw me: someone to talk to when you needed tickets to the prom. Maybe she was right. That's all our friendship had become. I was a connection.

"Andrew," I said, and already my voice grew bubbly, easy and light. As if I were grateful to be so shallow. "Wow. I never thought—"

"Don't 'Andrew Wow' me, all right?" She put her hands on her hips and stared at me contentiously. "We're just going to go together and have fun."

"I didn't mean anything—"

"I just thought it might be fun to go."

"I'm glad," I said. "I think it'll be a really wonderful—"

"Yeah, yeah." She waved her hand. "Save that for the little sorority sisters. When should I bring in the money?"

I told her as soon as possible and, awkwardly at first, we walked up the aisle of the auditorium together. "If you tease me about any of this," she mock-threatened, pointing her finger like a gun, "I'll kill you."

"Word of honor." I tried to smile. When we reached the hallway, Paula spied me, and waved me over to where she was laughing wildly with some friends.

"Hey," Madeline said. "I heard about Ridley. Congratulations."

I was off-balance, half my weight shifted in Paula's direction. "Thanks—I—"

"How come you didn't tell me?"

"I—I don't know." I stepped closer to her. "Because, I guess . . . you didn't get that scholarship, so—"

"So I don't go to the school I wanted to," Madeline said. "So what's that got to do with you?"

"I feel bad."

"Aw." She smiled a thin line. "Save it. Feeling bad doesn't do anything."

"I know," I said. And I looked away.

"Besides, I got into Atherton." She gave me a what-can-you-do shrug. "I guess I'm going there."

"Atherton," I mumbled. Then louder, "I'm happy for you."

At the corner of Elliot and Laurie streets, I huddled in a doorway with my collar up. It was a scene from a bad spy movie. First the note, with a crude map and Billy's handwriting: "Meet me Satur. morning. 9 am. important!!!"

Then Billy, slinking along the storefronts toward me, eyes darting all over.

Maybe he would just slip me a package with the secret formula inside, keep going as if he didn't know me, and the movie would end.

No such luck.

"Kerry!" he yelled from half a block away.

"This better be good," I threatened.

He gestured for me to follow him. "I saw you last night, at Pam Leach's party."

"I know, Billy. You talked to us, remember?"

He nodded, and sighed. "You and Kyle. You can tell something's wrong."

"Really," I said. And then, without intending to: "You can? What do you mean?"

"Just the way you stand next to each other. Like, not *really* talking. You know, like strangers."

I snapped, impatiently, "What did you want to show me?"

"Here. It's up here." He ran ahead a couple of storefronts, turned, and waited for me. "This place. Check it out."

I joined him, then stepped back to glance at the long sign over the display: Cavalier Formal Wear.

In the window were five or six dummies, each clad in a tuxedo topped with a crisp collar, bow tie, and the smooth circle of a headless neck.

"Guess which one I'm getting." Billy bounced from one foot to the other.

Most of the tuxes were black or white or a pin-striped gray, but in the corner there was one of wild, swirling paisley, as if the colors had had a nervous breakdown and were running amok. The whole tuxedo shimmered in the light from whatever angle you looked at it. The shirt was a pale lavender, with a waterfall of ruffles down the center. Beside the dummy was a black top hat and a glistening gold cane.

"Not that one," I said, and pointed, just to be sure.

"Is that outstanding, or what?"

"Words . . . can't do it justice. Billy . . ." Go on, tell him, I thought. Not even Billy Stockton deserved—

Then I saw his nose pressed against the glass as his eyes ran over every bit of the display. "It costs a little more, but I don't care," he murmured, still gazing at the tux. "Everybody thinks, you know, Billy Stockton, he's just a jock. Just a big jock, but no class. Good for some laughs, especially when he's with Kevin." His voice caught a little, and I saw his eyes shut, his face still against the window. "You know how I've felt since that goddamn garage?"

My throat caught, but he wasn't waiting for an answer.

"And how long I've been wanting to just feel good, even just for one night? Can you imagine when people see me in that—with you, Kerry? Even my friends, even the people who think they know me. . . .

"I can't wait," he said at last, turning to me.

But I was looking down, and for every word he said about the prom I forced myself to think of something else, to push his remorse from my mind. I had to remember the fire, of course, but not just that. How Madeline lost her scholarship. And what Billy said after the AIDS assembly. And then every dirty, racist, anti-Semitic, sexist, stupid joke he had ever told. I added up all his stunts, from all the parties this whole year, and how many chairs and mirrors he and Kevin had broken, how many carpets he had stained with beer, and most of all how many people he had hurt, and when I couldn't recall any more I started in again, repeating them, the way you force yourself to memorize something you can't afford to forget.

I shut my eyes, my brow against the glass. "I can't wait, either," I said.

20

We were on in two minutes, and Teddy wasn't there.

Mrs. McGann was in one of her frenzies at the front of the room, and I kept sending stealthy glances back to the door to search for him.

"As our school year draws to a close, the Author Projects," she said, "will be a true example of cooperative learning. . . ."

I *never* should have counted on him. What good was he, anyway? Mrs. McGann liked projects with a flair, and all we had was the *pfft* of a dud firecracker. First me, reading aloud to the class, then Teddy. Two separate, dull reports disguised as teamwork.

"You think maybe we can get a B minus out of this?" I had asked him in despair.

"Are you kidding? No way we don't get an A," he said.

I looked to the door again. Still no Teddy.

"Don't forget that in addition to your presentation," Mrs. McGann went on, "you owe a written report"—all around me the kids groaned, but she maintained her zesty smile—"in which you will detail the joys and difficulties of working with another person."

I raised my hand. "Mrs. McGann, if a person's partner doesn't show up, could there be an extension?"

"In that case," Mrs. McGann said, "the missing partner receives a zero, and the other partner must proceed as planned."

"But . . . what if . . . you see . . ."

"Coincidentally, Kerry, I believe your presentation is scheduled for today."

Teddy had volunteered us to go first—he and his "No way we don't get an A. . . ."

"Well then, Kerry, if you're ready, let's begin," she said as cordially as if she were inviting me to tea. I struggled to my feet, and just happened to catch the trace of a smile flutter across her face—a smile!

"Kerry Dunbar and Teddy Mattson," she announced, "on Thomas Hardy."

No, I said to myself, she couldn't be *smiling*. You're getting paranoid.

I trudged to the front of the room, bouncing off desks like a boat floating loose in a harbor. I stared at my notes until they became squiggles before my eyes. Maybe, just maybe, I could salvage a C. I took a deep breath and began. "Thomas Hardy," I croaked, "was a great English writer."

Okay, I could live with a D.

I read from my page, and after a couple of eternal minutes I looked up and saw my destiny. The vacant eyes. The doodling in the margins of notebooks. Well, why *should* they be interested? All I was doing was listing a lot of titles of books they had never read, and giving plot summaries, and babbling on how the critics said there was so much *deep symbolism* to the work.

And then I caught Mrs. McGann in the back of the room, without a doubt, *smiling*!

But still, it got worse. There was a sudden commotion at the door, and an old man stumbled in and almost knocked Mrs. McGann over. The class turned at the sound of his clumsy entrance, grateful for any kind of interruption. "Excuse me," he said, and coughed, taking what seemed like ten minutes to clear his throat. His graying hair was brushed straight back. He had a handlebar mustache, a tight, Edwardian-style high collar, and a pinched expression on his face.

He was heading straight for me.

Staggering, really, one hand reaching out to steady himself on the desks as he passed by, the other clutching a pile of old books.

"Ladies and gentlemen," Mrs. McGann announced, "please welcome Mr. Thomas Hardy."

He cleared his throat again and said, in a heavy English accent, "Quite an improvement on the old photo, what?" and he held out a picture from one of the books for the class to see. "Right. I thought I might add a word or two to what the young miss here has been saying about me. Set her straight on a few points."

He tottered up beside me. I mouthed, *I'll kill you.*

I spied a fleeting grin beneath Teddy's pancake makeup and mustache. But he only said, "Not interrupting your little book chat, am I?"

"No, no." I edged closer to my seat. "I was done, really. . . ." Now I felt all their eyes upon me. I glanced down to see that I had crumpled my notes into a thick wad. Mrs. McGann called out, "Just a little more, Kerry," and I heard the kids say "Yeah," "Come on," "More," wide awake now and loving this, and why shouldn't they? Weren't the Romans all perky and bright when they fed those Christians to the lions?

I read the rest quickly in a monotone with Thomas Hardy at my elbow. Once in a while the class snickered, and I knew he must have made some funny expression. As soon as I could I slumped to my seat.

"Just a minute, miss," Thomas Hardy called to me. "Or is it ms.?"

I waited long enough to load my answer with unmistakable scorn. "It's ms." I scowled.

"Don't I get an introduction?"

"And now," I bit off the words, "Mr. Thomas Hardy will speak about his life."

"Eh, eh, don't sit down just yet," he said. I hesitated in the middle of the aisle.

"Now, you know," he continued, "I've been listening to your report, and some of what you said was all well and good, but now that I have the chance . . . I'd like to ask—just how many of my books *have* you read?"

A ripple of laughter crossed the room.

"Three," I said. "Well, four. Almost." I looked down. "I didn't finish *Jude the Obscure*."

He reeled in shock. "You *didn't* . . . *finish* . . . *Jude the Obscure*. . . ."

The rest of the class caught on, and let out a collective mocking gasp. I saw myself up there, angry and trembling, too nervous to breathe, and Teddy and Mrs. McGann and all the class having such a great time, and I wondered, What the hell is wrong with me? I used to *love* doing stuff like this in school. Creative stuff. Silly stuff, where I could laugh and learn and not feel I had to look over my shoulder to see if I was drawing too much attention to myself. Now I stood like an outsider envying a happy group through a large window. What was wrong with me?

Nothing—I looked around and caught Madeline's eye— nothing I couldn't at least try to change.

"No, I didn't finish it," I said, dropping my gaze as if I were ashamed. Then I gave it back to him. "It was *boring*."

He peered at me as if his ears had failed him. *"Boring?"*

I fought back the grin. "That's right. Dull. Sleepy. Comaville."

"Young lady, it's . . . it's a *classic*." The class giggled, and he turned to them. "But you know," he said with stately puzzlement, "she's right. It *was* boring."

A spattering of applause. I inched closer to the dead author.

"Are you sure now," he said, "you read the other three? You *really* read them?"

"Of course," I said haughtily.

"You're sure you didn't just . . . oh, read the Cliffs Notes?"

I bit the inside of my cheek to keep a straight face while the class whooped.

"And what if I did?" I said. "Those plots of yours go on *forever*."

"Young lady, I was paid by the *word*."

"Next time I'm just going to rent the video."

We went on like that, bantering and bickering while the class took sides and cheered at a clever insult or a zinger of a comeback. They even asked questions on their own. It didn't take me long to realize we weren't just getting laughs and having fun, but Teddy was making me explain a lot of points I had made earlier, only more clearly, so the rest of the class could follow. He was making me *think* about Thomas Hardy, and be spontaneous, instead of just reading from my notes. I asked him why his women characters sometimes seemed so passive, and he talked about the lack of choices they had a hundred years ago. I teased him that his novels were outdated, and he gave examples of how they were still relevant today. And if once I had hoped just to stretch the report to ten minutes, now the bell interrupted us when it seemed we were only halfway through.

The class rose at their desks and gave us an ovation—it was pretty wild for AP kids. My eyes fell on Madeline. She stood, passionately applauding, her face red with approval.

Teddy grabbed me in a big bear hug, smearing me with his makeup and the spray-on gray from his hair.

"I will never, ever forgive you," I said, laughing.

"I couldn't tell you," he pleaded.

"Why not?"

"Because you would have been so *self-conscious*," he explained, "it wouldn't have worked. You would have been all concerned about your *image*."

"My image?"

He nodded.

"You're probably right," I agreed.

Mrs. McGann joined us at the front of the room. I couldn't even be mad at her for playing along with Teddy, she was so obviously proud of us. "You were both superb," she said. "Now I want you to capture that spontaneity in your report."

"That's *right*," I said, and looked at Teddy. "We have to do a written report."

"Oh no," Teddy groaned. "You mean I have to work with her *again*?"

My dress hung on the inside of the closet door, but by now I was long past losing myself in admiration for the fabric or the frilly lace along the hem. The closer and closer I got to the prom, the more the dress seemed to belong to someone else. I halfway expected it to take form on its own, for a face to appear, a face hardened and cynical that would scold me for my second thoughts.

The floorboards creaked. There was my mother in the doorway of my room. She wasn't more than a step or two inside, and I felt embarrassed, caught staring at my dress this way. I said, "I was just—"

"I'm sorry," she spoke at the same time. "I didn't mean to—"

"What?" I asked.

"No, it's okay. . . ." She pulled away.

Say something, I thought.

"It was nothing important," she said, and in an instant she was gone from my door.

I had a glimpse of that morning in Mrs. McGann's class, of

my panicky moment when everything was closing in on me, and how the only way out was to wrench my backbone straight and do just what I didn't think I could, take on Teddy, and the class—and myself—and triumph.

This time I followed my mother down the hall.

She was on the stairs already. I called, "Mom," and when she didn't respond I stood at the top and said the first thing I thought of.

"I'm sorry your project didn't get accepted."

She froze, and I knew I had to go on before I backed down.

"I think—I think it's really shitty the way it turned out."

She might have said, Don't curse, at least. But she didn't even look up. "It's all right," she mumbled.

"It's *not* all right." I caught up to her where she lingered at the bottom step. "And it's not all right for you to brood, either. You should be angry."

"I don't see the point when—"

"You realize you haven't said a thing to me about it in all this time? Aren't you just livid? That they turned down such a good program?"

She didn't know whether to sit or to run. She backed up against the banister, cornered. "Kerry, why should it bother you? You've got . . ."

"What?"

"Your friends, and *Kyle*." It was as harsh as she could make it. "And your busy, busy social life—"

"There's room for you in it, if you want to be!" I shouted. "Mom, did you ever once go to the county supervisor—"

"Enough about that." Then, after a second, "You can't just walk in and see him—"

"Did you ever try?"

"He's got aides and consultants and yes-men—"

"*Did you ever try?* You didn't, did you? You just said, 'I

can't win,' and that's that. Do you think Dad would just go around sulking?"

"Of course not, your father has gone through so many jobs—"

"Sure, and he always bitches and moans, but at least he tells you how he feels."

I lost her with that one. She was off the stairs and into the living room, grabbing some files from an end table and curling onto the corner of the sofa. She sighed and shook her head as she always did to signal she had work to do, but this time I wasn't letting her get away. I climbed onto the sofa and sat beside her. I could feel where the sharp, broken shaft of the frame protruded in the center, and I slid my butt around it. We were wedged together.

"This sofa can't hold two people anymore—"

"Then we'll fix it," I said.

She threw down her files. "Has it ever occurred to you that your father and I are just a bit different?"

"Of course you are. But are you just going to feel sorry for yourself the rest of your life?" In the lamplight I saw the glitter of tears. "Mom, you were never right for Dad. And he wasn't right for you. Dad's—Dad thinks he's twenty years old."

"And I'm a middle-aged woman getting older."

"Stop feeling sorry for yourself. I didn't say it was *good* he thinks he's twenty. It just shows it never would have lasted between you two. If it was meant to, he'd still be here, wouldn't he?"

Silently she started to cry. I was actually scared at first. It was so strange of her. I thought furiously of a dozen things to do to make her stop. I could apologize. Run off to find tissues. Take a hint and leave her alone as she wanted, go to my room for an hour or so.

In the end I let her cry. I laid my hand on her shoulder gently.

"What makes you such an expert?" she sniffed. She even half smiled.

I hugged her. It wasn't easy, either, perching on the sharp wreckage of the sofa.

"I think I know," I whispered through my own tears, "I think I know if people belong together. . . ."

21

As it turned out I was grateful that on the night before the prom I had to meet with Teddy at the library and finish our written report. Better that than pace around my house and stare from clock to clock like a prisoner on execution eve. By the time I got to the library—I had seen a Chrysler I thought was Billy's, and hidden for ten minutes in somebody's bushes—it was just after six. I took a prominent seat and tried to calm myself. By now I was prepared for just about any outfit of Teddy's. Fireman? Indian chief? Big Bird? He could show up dressed like an amoeba—I didn't put it past him—and I wouldn't even blink.

But when he arrived, ten minutes later, loping along in that loony duck waddle of his, I was the only one in the library to stare. His blond hair was washed and fluffy. No headbands, no braids. His face was ruddy. He was wearing sneakers, jeans without any holes or messages written in red ink, and a baggy but unremarkable gray Yale sweatshirt.

The first thing I said was, "I thought you were going to Cornell."

"I am," he answered, looking down at the lettering on his chest. "That's the point."

But the real point was that Teddy looked pretty normal. He even looked good.

"Sorry I'm late," he said. "These extraterrestrials stopped me for directions—"

Looks, of course, could be deceiving. "Let's just get to work."

He examined me carefully. "Boy, you're a mess."

"Thanks. I don't feel frazzled enough without your telling me."

"Aren't you excited about the prom tomorrow?" he asked.

"Sure I am," I said, in the tone of the dead. "Can we work?"

"I *just . . . can't . . . believe*"—he sounded so compassionate—"this project is due the day of the prom."

"Why do you care?" I asked sharply, and tried to keep the envy out of my voice. "You're not going."

"Hey, I still care. Aren't you tense, with the prom tomorrow? Aren't you nervous?" He escalated his voice dramatically. "Aren't you going *out of control*?"

"Stop it!"

"Thomas Hardy: A Report." He spoke dramatically, like a news announcer. I scrambled to get down the first few lines as he began dictating—until I realized he was teasing me here, too. His voice had reverted to a fourth-grade monotone, like a kid copying something from the encyclopedia. When I looked up he was grinning naughtily.

"You're a jerk," I said.

"Come on. Let's get out of here. Let's do this somewhere else."

"No, we're here, we don't have too much time—"

"Please? Please?" He squirmed down off his chair, knelt before me, and gazed up with wide-open eyes. "I have a real good reason."

I shook my head in disgust, but I couldn't keep back the smile. "All right, all right." I gathered my books. On the way to his battered Volkswagen Teddy bounced happily beside me. It was like taking a sheepdog for a walk. "Where are we going?" I asked briskly. "And what's your real good reason?"

At the first red light he showed me. He withdrew a plastic pink bottle he had wedged in his pocket, unscrewed the top, fished out a little wand, and blew steadily until a silvery bubble emerged. Teddy leaned his head out the window. The bubble caught the breeze and took shape like a butterfly leaving a cocoon. It grew. And grew. Soon it was nearly two feet across before it broke free of the wand and wafted away.

"*Did you see the size of that one?*" he yelped.

"Teddy, you're nuts. You're certifiable."

"I mixed some glycerin in, they really get huge—"

"*That* was your reason we had to leave?"

"What, I'm supposed to blow bubbles in the *library*?"

"Of course not, but—"

"So wasn't it a good reason?"

"Teddy," I said, laughing, "when you start making sense it scares me."

"I am totally logical," he insisted, even as the truck driver in the next lane started cursing at us when the bubble floated inside his cab. "It's the rest of the world that's crazy."

"You may be right," I sighed. "So where are we going?"

But he wouldn't tell me. First he talked about bubble surface tension. From there he moved to snorkel clubs in the Gobi Desert. He ended up playing a tape of a band I'd never heard. I didn't even notice our destination until he parked the car.

"We're going to the *mall*?" I said.

"Uh-huh." He wrenched the emergency brake and hopped out.

"Teddy, one thing I know you are not is a mall rat. And besides, we have to get this report done—"

"We will." He grabbed my hand and yanked me along.

Now I had been to malls about five thousand times in my

life—but I had never been to one with Teddy Mattson. It wasn't just a mall to him; it was a grand arcade, a combination of the Olympics and Walt Disney World.

"Ooh, watch this, watch." He pulled me to a halt a few yards away from a mother and her six-year-old son. They stood just outside a toy store. "You're just in time for the semifinals of the Can I Nag a Toy Out of Mom When She Has No Intention of Buying Me Anything?" As the boy tugged his mother, despite all the times she yelled *no,* toward the toy store, we struggled to hide our hysterics. When she finally gave up and followed him inside, Teddy threw up his hands. "We have a winner!"

We went on like that: we watched guys go up to strange girls in what Teddy called the Pickup Sweepstakes. While mothers and fathers bickered we chose winners in the One Big Happy Family Contest. By the time Teddy had us settled at a table in the food court I had almost forgotten about the report. We got out the paper and started half a dozen times, each sentence crumbling before we finished it. We laughed at how bad it sounded, how pretentious.

"I know," I said. "Let's make it like a sociology report." Teddy looked on. As I recited aloud in serious tones, I wrote it down. "The Author Project unites young people of various"—I pondered—"of various sociological orientations. . . ."

"Ooohh," Teddy purred. "That's good. Let's grub for that A."

I steered us on from there, loading in so much crap we ended up giggling our way through the whole report, and if it wasn't good, at least it was fun. Afterward we sat back, drained, and shared a pizza.

"You know, Teddy," I said, after he had gobbled down his half in about a minute and was eyeing mine, "you're nothing like I thought you were."

"You're not, either. I always wondered, well . . ."

"What?"

"Well, why you hang around with"—he stole an olive from my side of the pizza as he said it—"the kind of people you hang around with. You know, the party animals, the jocks"—he threw up his hands—"not that I don't like sports."

"Oh, of course you do," I said. "Especially cheerleading." At the mention of his prank he reached up to pat at his eyebrow, though by now all the cuts had healed. "You mean Linda, right? And Heather Grady." I held back a second before I said it. "And . . . Billy Stockton, and . . ."

He nodded.

"I don't know, just—we're friends. Simple as that." He laid his cheek on a fist and watched me, and something about those warm green eyes, that goofy cuteness, made it seem I could tell him anything. Okay, so it was Teddy Mattson, a lunatic. The world surprised you sometimes. "They're my friends," I repeated. "They know things about me that nobody . . . should know."

"Exactly," he gently mocked me, "what friends are for."

"And I . . . I know things about them. So the more—we're together . . ."

"The less chance to tell somebody else."

His tone was so unexpectedly bright that I agreed, eagerly. "That's right."

"So here"—he leaned in, darting looks around—"you're with me. They're not around." He narrowed his eyes and whispered, *"Tell me."*

I pulled back, away from him. "I can't."

"Come on."

"You're just making fun—"

"Of course I am. I always do." He shrugged. "That doesn't mean I'm not serious."

"No," I said. "I need to tell someone else . . . first."

"So practice on me." He nodded at the idea. "I'll be that other person. Guy or girl?"

"A girl. But there's a guy, too."

"So let me be the guy." He tilted his head, goofing on some dashing Romeo from a daytime soap.

"There's no way," I said with a laugh, "you could ever be him." Teddy looked as hurt as a puppy. "Sorry. I didn't mean that to be nasty. It's just that"—I looked down—"you're so different. . . ."

"From him?"

"Definitely."

"How about you? Am I different from you?"

"Teddy"—I tried to make light of it—"you're different from the whole human race. . . ." But he heard me straining too hard.

"But am I different from you?" he asked again quietly.

"I don't know. Because I guess I don't know . . . who I am." I shook my head. "I spent this whole year trying to find out."

Teddy helped me finish my slices. We wandered through the mall again.

"What's the next event?" I asked halfheartedly.

"Couples in Love," Teddy announced grandly.

"How depressing."

"Come on," he chided me. "Where's your sporting spirit?" He hurried us onto the escalator, surveying the bottom level as we descended. "Look, hand-holding." He nodded to a man and woman in their early twenties. "Definitely early stage."

"Mmm, early to middle," I estimated, straight-faced.

"Maybe mid-middle," he said; then, "Oooh, oooh, look." He pointed to a small group of high school guys, and one impatient girl who stood a few feet off. "He's ignoring her for his buddies."

"Definitely late stage there," I said.

Teddy turned to me; "Terminal." And we laughed.

"I think I understand the rules," I said.

Outside a hair salon we saw Diane Penske, a girl from school, whispering frantically to a friend. She stared at her reflection in the display window, tugging at her new perm in panic. Her friend tried to console her.

"Aha," Teddy mused. "Could be a case of Prom Anxiety here."

At the mention of the prom I felt the smile slide from my face.

He noticed immediately. "What's wrong?"

"Nothing."

For a moment he watched me closely.

"You know," he said, "I kind of wish I was going to the prom."

"I wish you were, too."

"What are you going to wear?" he asked.

"Just . . . some dress."

"Now if *I* were going, what would I wear?" he wondered.

We passed a party favors store, and I pointed to a six-foot cardboard cutout of a clown. "There," I teased. "That's you."

"No." He acted wounded. "This is the prom. This is *serious*. I'd do it right." We stopped in the middle of the mall and he held my arm while he wrinkled his brow in contemplation. "Tails," he said at last.

"You mean like a really formal outfit?"

"Yeah, I'd be proper. I'd wear one of those tuxes with tails. And a prim little tie. And cuff links that glitter when the light shines on them. . . ."

"Teddy, what are you talking about? You'd never come to the prom like that."

"Yes, I would."

"You'd come in, oh, a tie-dyed tux with ostrich feathers in your headband, and . . . and . . ."

"Yeah?" He was amused. "Keep going."

"And a little Christmas ornament as an earring, a

Mickey Mouse watch, probably some tin cans dragging on the ground behind you, and—and a coin changer on your belt—"

"So that's," he challenged, "how you see me?"

I thought about it and smiled. "Yes."

"So Teddy Mattson doesn't have a romantic side. . . ."

"I didn't say that, but—"

"And whoever went with me would have to suffer through total embarrassment—"

"I didn't say that, either—"

"—because Teddy Mattson doesn't know the first thing about romance."

"I—"

The next thing I knew he was kissing me. A big kiss, too, kind of clumsy and wet, and I was kissing back.

It felt as if it lasted ten years—or at least a minute.

Finally we broke apart.

"Wooo-eeee," he said, and whistled. "Now, that's romance."

His words stung me like a slap. "You make fun of everything."

"Who said I was making fun?"

"You just *did*."

"Wait a minute. Kissing's not *fun*?"

"That's not what I meant—"

"Think about it. It's not only fun, it's funny. Lips pressed together. Real *serious* expressions. And nobody can breathe just right. It always makes me think of goldfish. Or lifeguards, giving CPR."

I tightened my lips to hold back a smile.

"Besides," he said. "People laugh when they're . . . nervous."

"*You're* nervous?" I felt dizzy, but somehow brave. "Dressing up like a *cheerleader* is okay, but *kissing* makes you nervous?"

He slipped his arm around my shoulder. "Kissing you"—
he blushed—"a little . . ."

"If people were watching us," I said as we strolled along,
"what stage would this be?"

"Hmm." He pretended to give it deep thought. "That's a
good one. Early?"

"*Early* early." I grinned. "If that."

Over the piped-in music system a syrupy tune came on. I
groaned at the corny strings. Not Teddy. He paused, listened
as if angels whispered to him, and lunged for me so abruptly
that for a second I was startled. He took my hand and pulled
me close. Then we were dancing, there in the main thorough-
fare of the mall. Teddy hummed along dreamily. At first I
wriggled to be free, thinking it was more of his mockery and I
had fallen for it again. Shoppers and couples and families
passed, and a few looked at us as we swirled around a display
of kitchenware. Most stepped politely aside as if they didn't
even see us. I stopped struggling, figuring he would tire of it
soon, but once I stopped resisting he drew me closer. His
grasp grew softer, more tender. We were really dancing by
now. He was still humming, his lips at my ear. We whirled on.
We seemed to avoid bumping into potted plants and baby
strollers as if by magic. I felt his hand at the small of my back,
and I laid my head on his shoulder. I even shut my eyes and
let myself follow him, drifting with him, the sounds of the
mall fading away until all that was left was the comforting
murmur of a melody from his throat, his touch, and (I could
feel myself smiling) his scent—the scent of giant, slippery
soap bubbles. I held him tighter.

At last we stopped. He brought my hand to his lips and
kissed it.

"That's what I'd do at the prom," he said.

From the second level people applauded us. Some whistled and cheered.

"Anyway, I should get you home."

"What—what about the report?" I protested. "It's still . . . rough."

"Here, I'll take it." He crumpled it up and stuffed it in a pocket. "I'll type it up."

"I can do it," I said.

"No, no, no." He shook me lightly by the shoulders. "You've got the prom tomorrow. You've got a lot to think about tonight."

"Do I ever," I agreed.

22

Don't be stupid, I thought.

I lay in bed, somewhere between midnight and dawn.

Just go. How many girls would die to be with Kyle tomorrow night?

I looked at my clock radio. Tomorrow was already today.

Just go. Suffer Billy's anger. Sort things out afterward. You smile and you dance and everyone says how good you look and deep down you know how envious they are of you—

So when does it start to mean something?

At one point I must have fallen asleep. I only know because once I started, and leaped up. At the foot of my bed I saw a figure looming—

"Mom?" I cried.

Someone else. Some stranger—

But it was only the prom dress on my closet door. In the breeze, the plastic rippled faintly across it.

I didn't sleep anymore after that. I counted down with the clock and got up at five-thirty, padded quietly to the bathroom, showered and dressed, and was out of the house without my mother stirring.

It wasn't yet six-thirty by the time I approached Kyle's house. I stood at the edge of the lawn, in the shelter of a tree, and then lurked around until I located his bedroom window.

At first I was going to tap, but I brought my hand up just short of the glass. Rising up on my toes, I peered in.

Kyle's room was huge. Over the desk was a Layton pennant, and a framed blowup of an article highlighting his season. There was a stack of college catalogs next to the phone, and in the corner a couple of basketballs and four or five pairs of high-top athletic shoes. The room was so large you could whisper something from the bed at one end and a person at the other end wouldn't hear your whisper at all. You'd have to say it louder to be heard, and maybe it was the type of thing you didn't want to raise your voice to say. So in the end you said nothing.

I leaned in closer, pressing the side of my face against the glass so I could see along the wall closest to me. Soon I was contorted, my hands propped against the window frame and all my weight on one leg.

"You have to be," the voice said, "the most uncomfortable-looking prowler I have ever seen."

I fell back from the window into Kyle's mom.

"Oh," I said, embarrassed. "I'm just—I had to—I'm—"

"Looking for Kyle?" She smiled. "Big night, tonight. I'll bet you can't wait."

I tried to grin back. She put me so at ease I wanted to stand there forever, pretending everything she said was true.

"Come on in." She motioned to the patio door. "Had your breakfast?"

My voice sounded scratchy. "I couldn't eat."

"Too excited, hmm?" I followed her to the kitchen. It had the efficient, industrial look of a factory. Sunlight glittered off the chrome-and-white furnishings. "Well," Mrs. West said with a laugh, "no such problems for Mr. Romantic here."

Kyle, wearing a deep red velour robe, was settled at the round glass table, hunched over a bowl of cereal. Beside it stood a large orange box.

Mrs. West left us, and I smiled in spite of myself. "I might have known you'd eat Wheaties."

"Yeah." He swallowed. "What's up?"

I moved to sit across from him, but only got as far as resting my full weight on the back of the chair. If I started out with short, little words, maybe I could work my way up to . . .

Kyle's eyes drifted to the sports page.

I stared at my white knuckles on the chair back. "Look. I've been waiting . . . a long time . . ."

He glanced up from his cereal.

". . . for this all—"

"Wait a minute. For what?"

"—to mean something. To mean more to me. . . ."

At last he was alert, as if I were an intriguing news item on television.

"I've been waiting for all the time we've spent together . . . and everything"—I looked at him—"we do—together, and all we know about each other . . ."

"I have no idea what you're talking about," he said.

"Kyle, it should add up to more."

He inclined his head. That was all. And in the pause while he peered at me curiously, I thought, Now. Go on. Say it.

What came out was something else.

"Listen." I sat down across from him. "You know . . . last November. You remember when Madeline Abraham's garage burned down?"

No response—just the merest wrinkling of his brow. "Yeah?"

"Kyle—it was my fault."

His face changed rapidly. His eyes went wide, and I could almost see my words race up to his brain and trigger a meaning there. "You?"

I nodded, biting my lip.

"I thought it was Billy and Kevin."

I looked up, stunned. "You heard—you knew—"

"At least that's what Kevin told me."

I mumbled, "We weren't supposed to tell *anyone*...."

"I'm surprised Billy didn't tell me," Kyle said. "Give him a few beers and there's nothing he'll hold back."

Not quite, I thought. I said, "I can't believe you've known all along and you never once mentioned it."

"I didn't see how it mattered to us. What do you mean, it was your fault?"

"Kyle, I was there."

He held his hands out, palms up. "So?"

"So? So I'm *responsible*."

"Wait a minute, come on. It was Billy and Kevin jerking around, right?"

He held my gaze until I agreed.

"You didn't do anything. So"—he leaned forward and explained in a tone of weary expertise, as if the world out there had its own rules and behavior, and I was a little slower in learning them than he'd given me credit for—"the best thing to do is keep your mouth shut about it."

"I have. Don't you see?" I heard my voice rev up a notch. "I haven't even told Madeline."

"Hell, I hope not. You shouldn't have even told *me*."

"Not told you? But I *had* to...."

"Why?" He waited, as if I were really supposed to answer that. "Has it changed anything, telling me?"

"No." I sighed. "It hasn't changed anything."

"See? So don't—"

"But Kyle, what about you? Don't you see me differently? Don't you think bad of me?"

"For what?" He shook his head. "For just being there?"

"For that," I said, "but worse, for not doing anything about it later."

"Ker"—his voice was only a mild scolding—"you've got to forget about it."

"But I *can't.*"

"Look. You can't *unburn* it. You can't change what happened. So you learn to forget it. They had insurance, right? That's what insurance is *for,* to make mistakes okay."

"That's what Linda told me."

"Well, Linda knows how things work."

And I didn't. I looked up.

Kyle said, "What are you *crying* for?"

I was. But it was odd: there were tears, but no sobbing, no stinging. I could hardly feel them.

"The garage," I said. "The fire." I smiled weakly. "That's not even what I came to tell you." I took a deep breath. "Kyle, I don't want to go to the prom."

"What is it, that toast you have to make? I told you, don't worry—"

"No, I mean, I don't want to go with you."

The words seemed trapped beneath the high ceiling of the kitchen. For a second there was no expression of any kind on his face. Then he did the worst thing. He grinned. "Ha ha," he said.

"I'm not joking. I'm sorry. I know I've waited too long to tell you."

"Hold on. You're serious about this?"

I felt a deep ache way down in my stomach.

"I don't get it," he said. Then, suspiciously, "What the hell do you want from me?"

"What do I *want* from you?"

"People just don't . . . *call off* things like this without a good reason."

"That's *right,*" I said, "you see?"

"So what are you doing this for?"

"I'm—I'm doing it for me, Kyle."

For an instant he was flustered, then annoyed. "That's not a reason."

I said, "I don't want you to be hurt—"

"Hurt?"

"But I can't hide the truth about how I feel."

"Kerry, we have to go through this the morning of the prom?"

"Maybe it's more what I *don't* feel. . . ."

"Okay, so tell me, what is it you don't feel?"

"I can't"—I brought my hands up helplessly, as if I could shape something he might understand—"I can't just answer you like that."

"Tell me!" He slammed his fist on the table. The bowl and glass danced. Then he calmed to a scary intensity. "Just tell me what you don't feel." I groped for words. "You can't, can you? Because you're so screwed up, you can't see what's right in front of you."

What was right in front of me was an image of Teddy, holding and spinning me in lazy, graceful circles at the mall.

"What I feel—"

"Don't tell me it's this condom thing, still. I thought you gave up on—"

"No. It's not that. It's not that at all." I shoved my hands beneath the table to hide the trembling. "It's—I don't love you, Kyle."

He leaned toward me, incredulous. "Since when are we talking about love?"

It gave me time to draw a breath, and find his eyes. "That's what I mean."

"Kerry, we go to the prom, we have a great time, we talk about this stuff later—"

"I'm sorry."

He reached out his hand and fiddled with the spoon, the glass, the cereal box.

"Sorry is right," he said.

"I'll pay you back for your prom ticket. And anything else, if you lose any deposits. . . ."

"Why don't you get the hell out of here," he said.

"I'm wrong, I know, for waiting so long to tell you—but I just—"

"Get out!" His tone warned me first. I pushed back from the chair, fumbled my way to the door. *"Get out!"* he yelled again. I turned to speak and only half dodged the Wheaties box he flung at me. It clipped my right cheek and ricocheted off a cabinet, and for a moment the air exploded with a thousand flakes of brown, and then I was out on his lawn, running across the wet grass, running home.

I showered again, and changed, and by the time the trembling stopped I knew I'd be late for first period, so I figured I'd miss it altogether and compose myself. My mother, who was riding her bicycle to work in the warm weather, had already left. In the bathroom mirror I saw a pale girl with eyes puffy from lack of sleep.

By the time I left for school I was half-delirious. My first walk down the corridor was torture. I tried to lose myself in the crowds, but all I imagined was the word of what I'd done, circulating faster than light, and I dreaded turning some corner and finding Kyle, finding anyone who knew me. I kept my eyes to the floor; once or twice I heard my name called and pretended I didn't. I took shallow, frequent breaths, as if the school were running low on oxygen.

I sat through my morning classes, barely listening. All I worried about was finding Teddy. When lunch came I decided to seek him out. It wasn't easy. I had to do a circuit of the school, but when I did find him he was in a logical enough spot, for Teddy. He was at the edge of the field behind the school, about twenty feet off the ground. His legs encircled a stout branch of an oak tree while he inched out toward the end, his right arm extended.

"Teddy," I called.

"Ssshhhhhh."

"Teddy, come down, okay?"

"I can't. You climb up."

"Climb up?" I hadn't climbed a tree since—

I looked around. A boy with binoculars leaned against a car, following Teddy's every move. Three other kids stood behind him. Another handful was gathering farther back, and someone ran between the groups, marking down notes on a pad of paper.

I stood at the bottom, appraising the knotty trunk. "Teddy. Couldn't you just—"

"Is it important?"

"Yes."

"Then you'd better climb up. I probably won't be down for a while."

All right. I hauled myself up, level with him, too nervous to look down. He was way out toward the end of the branch. "Teddy. What's this all about?"

Ever so slowly he tilted his head back my way. "See that squirrel?" At the far end of the branch a wary squirrel bobbed up and down. "I bet Donny Sinclair I could get it to take this Snickers before the bell rings."

Down below, I realized, they were betting on Teddy's chances.

"Last night was fun," he said.

That might have been my best chance. "Teddy. How would you . . ." I inched further along the branch. "Will you go to the prom with me?"

He didn't say anything at first. Slowly the branch began to sway.

"Did you hear me?"

"I'm speechless."

"Well, *that's* a first," I teased. This would work, I knew, if I could only get him laughing, if we treated it like the biggest joke in the world. "I want you to go with me," I said.

"Kerry?"

"What?"

"Do you think if I made, like, squirrel sounds, I could get it—"

"*Teddy.*"

He pulled up and revolved around the branch, clinging to the underside like a sloth. At last he faced me. The squirrel retreated to the far tip, but didn't yet leap away.

"Aren't you going with your athlete friend?"

"I broke it off," I said.

"Time's running out!" Donny Sinclair yelled from below.

Cautiously, I turned to look down. There were probably fifteen kids now, shading their eyes against the sun to watch us.

"I broke it off because—because he *wasn't* a friend."

"But why do you want to go with me?"

"Because . . . you are. Does that make sense?"

He didn't answer.

"People see Kyle and me, and they think I'm a certain type of person, you know? And I'm not. I know it's not me they're seeing—"

"It's not."

"No. And if they—if they saw me with you, they'd be—"

"They'd have a better idea of the real you."

"*Exactly.*" I sighed with relief.

"If you went with me, and they saw us together, who would they think you are then?"

"I—I'd be who I always was." I struggled to say, "The way I want to be again."

I wanted to be near enough for him to hug me, like last night, but he was out of arm's reach and there was no way I was crawling out any more. "I just thought . . ." I heard my voice rise up a notch. "Can't you just go with me?"

"It's not that simple."

"It is!" I shouted. "We get dressed up, we go. . . ."

He shook his head. "All I hear from you is what people will see, and what they'll think." He swung his leg over and looked at me. "Why don't you forget about what they'll think?"

"I guess"—I looked down at the ground—"that's not so easy."

He leaned toward me, the squirrel forgotten. "Look. Last night was our prom."

I was getting dizzy now and no spot on the branch seemed quite steady enough.

"You liked it, didn't you?"

"I loved it, damn you."

"I did, too," he said. "You know why? Because it just happened. There wasn't anybody watching—"

"There was the whole *mall*."

"And you didn't care about impressing a single one of them, did you?"

"If you only knew"—my voice wavered—"what I've done today. . . ."

"Hey, I thought a lot about last night—"

"I've done more than think!" I snapped. "Can't you just rent some tux and go with me?" Oh, why couldn't he pull something goofy from his pocket like a squirt gun, or squeak like Mickey Mouse, to make me laugh?

Instead he said, "Look. Last night—remember how you said you couldn't practice on me? It wouldn't be the same?"

"I remember I kissed you. That wasn't practice." My voice grew shrill. "That was the real thing."

"I know." He clutched the branch. "My taking you to the prom wouldn't be."

I whispered, "I can't believe you'd let me down like this."

"Kerry—I'd really let you down if I said yes."

Then I was scrabbling down the tree, burning my hands on the bark. I leaped the last six feet, staggering to keep my balance on the ground. Donny Sinclair lowered his binoculars to look at me.

"Too bad." He sounded disappointed. "I was hoping you could get him down."

"Not a chance," I mumbled. In the distance I could hear the sounds of the school: the bell clanging, footsteps on the stairs, lockers slamming shut, and voices, overwhelming everything else, voices high, lilting, laughing—

I doubled back, through the woods next to the school so I wouldn't have to pass the Senior Steps, and only when I emerged on a quiet side street did I stop, bend over for breath, and will myself to look calm.

After a block, I thought, Now where?

Where else? Home. And now it made sense to me, home, and a life like my mother's. That's what I would do, in the last few days of school that were left. Lug my work home, shut the door, curl up somewhere and block it all out until I fell asleep where I sat, get up the next day, do it again.

I felt better then, inside and out. Like when the dentist works on a cavity and your jaw gets numbed with Novocain.

And then it came to me. What a fool I was. I still had a date, if I wanted one. I had Billy Stockton.

Just go with Billy. Then there'd be no loose ends. Let him have the night of his life in his silly tux. Let him sip the secret beers he'd stash away, I'd smile and dance every dance with him, until the notion of running to the police was buried deep within him, too deep to ever surface. I could solve everything, that way. I could give the toast in a strong, confident voice. Let them whisper about me all night, *She dumped Kyle West, did you know that?* I'd shrug it off.

If it was that, or live my mother's life, the choice was clear.

By this time I was pacing through my house, and it wasn't until my fortieth tour of the kitchen that I spotted the note she had left me. Call your father, with his work number scrawled beneath it. I did one more circuit, trying to clear my head. Okay. Call Dad. Get it over quickly. Then get ready. Billy at seven-thirty.

It was that simple.

Up in my mother's bedroom the message light was glowing on the phone machine. I rewound and listened. Kyle's voice lunged at me fiercely.

"Hey, bitch, I just wanted to let you know you don't have to shed any tears for me, not that you would anyway, 'cause it didn't take long to line up somebody else, I guess somebody else knows a good deal when she sees it so the hell with you—"

The machine finally beeped him off. I sat for a minute or so, almost forgetting about my father. I tried at the real estate office, then got him on his car phone. I heard, "Jack Dunbar, homefinder," through the static.

"Hi, honey," he sang out when he recognized my voice.

"Dad, I don't have a lot of time, I'm really stressed out—"

"It's the weekend—why aren't you relaxing?"

"It's the prom. Remember? And if you only knew what today was like—"

"Oh my God," he said suddenly, and his tone went flat. "I forgot about the prom. Oh boy."

"Dad, what is it?"

"Look, Kerry, if tonight's the prom I'll just call you back later, maybe after the weekend, and—"

"Dad."

"It's not important, it's—" Even on such a poor connection I swore I heard him swallow. "No. No, I'm not going to do that," he said, as if talking to himself. "Kerry, I'm just going to say what I have to say, without any baloney. Okay?"

"Okay."

"You know—about my finances . . ."

"Uh, not exactly," I said warily.

"My expenses, I should say. Well, alimonies. You know, to Lynn."

And Claudette, I thought. And Mom. "Yeah."

"And"—his voice went inaudible for a second—"uh, child

support . . . and the market, you know the housing market's going through a—what we call a *sluggish* period. . . ."

"Dad. What are you saying?"

"Well—it looks like—I think we're going to have to hold off on Ridley right now, Kerry."

I got incredibly absorbed with a little gummy smudge just above the number 4 on the phone.

"Kerry? I'm sorry to have to tell you today—"

"Um-hmm," I droned softly.

"But I think I owe you the truth."

"The truth," I said.

"You know," he went on, and his voice picked up some enthusiasm, "maybe the financial aid office could have another look at your case."

"They already turned me down."

"I'll give them a call, and—"

"No, Dad—*they turned me down*. Let's be *honest* about it. I mean, as long as we're being so *goddamn honest*."

Silence. Then, "I'm sorry, Kerry. I know you're disappointed. I am, too. But look, we've still got Atherton. I'll bet it's not such a bad school, when you get right down to it. . . ."

I let him go on for a while, until I laid the receiver down gently and sat in total silence.

At some point the phone rang, loud and jarring. I stepped back and didn't answer it. I was too intrigued by the girl in the mirror by my mother's bedroom door. What an eerie face she had. Streaked with silent tears. Calm and wretched at once. With all the time in the world, and not a second to lose. I marveled at her composure. How long could she stay that way, without cracking? I stood and watched.

It didn't take so long at that.

23

....

There were a million things I was supposed to do that afternoon: try on my dress, go over the toast I had to read, call Paula and tell her once again, It's all going to work out fine.

What I did was go to see Rhonda.

I left my mother a note that I had the car and was heading to Rhonda's, and I just drove. Yes, I ran away. Rhonda's school was four to five hours north, and I had never really driven that far on my own before, but there was enough gas to get started and I thought I had enough money for more and within the first fifteen minutes, once I hit the highway out of town and the speedometer nudged seventy and my hair was whipping back, I felt great. If there was one person who knew who I really was, knew how to straighten me out when I was so jumbled up, it was Rhonda. I wanted her to pat my hand and reassure me that the world was no scarier now than it ever had been.

Rhonda lived off campus, and I kept taking wrong turns and backing up in strange driveways. My hair was gummy and all over the place. I didn't care. Maybe Brad would be there. We'd sit in the middle of her living room and I'd tell them everything. Yes, everything. At last, the chance to tell it all.

It was just eight o'clock by the time I found her apartment complex. Taking a deep breath, I climbed the stairs to the second-floor address and knocked loudly. "Hey Rhonda, open up," I called, too exhausted to care how loud I was. I knocked again, and heard footsteps.

For the first time in hours, I thought of the prom.

I saw the guys in their tuxes, the girls in glitzy gowns—

You look so fabulous!

—heard the squeals of delight—

Here, get a picture of us, here!

Come on, I told myself, think of something clever to say to Rhonda, and why was I *crying,* of all things, as I knocked harder and harder, *shaking* as my knuckles began to ache—

The door pulled back, and there she was. She looked wonderful: her cheeks full of color, her figure trim in a light spring dress.

I smiled. Who needed to be clever? "Rhonda. It's me."

Only her eyes seemed different. Puzzled. I saw that, for a second, at least, she had not recognized me.

"It's Kerry," I said.

"Kerry," she mumbled, dazed, and peered closer. Then *"Kerry,"* and she hugged me. "What are you *doing* here?"

"I have so much to tell you," I jabbered as she pulled me inside. I sank into the nearest chair.

"How'd you get here?" she asked. "Do you have a car?"

"My mother's car," I said in something close to a laugh. "I stole it. Now I'm a car thief, too."

"What do you mean, 'too'?" she said, but I was already on to the prom, on to Kyle and Teddy and how I never wanted to run the damn prom in the first place—

"Wait a minute. Slow down." Rhonda sat for a while, tried to follow, then sprang up. I hardly noticed. I told her about Ridley and my father's call, and Billy—

"Wait—which one is Billy?"

"It wasn't really cruel," I told her, "he had it coming—"

I wasn't making sense, I knew, and I knew I had to go way,

way back, even before *Jew him around* and Jessica's party, back to November—

"Kerry, listen," Rhonda said.

—back where I always ended up, back where all my stories started from—

At the first mention of Madeline's garage Rhonda stopped fidgeting. She sat and stared, as if afraid to move.

"Are you sure you should be telling me this?"

"Of course I'm sure," I stammered madly.

"You broke into her garage?" She looked incredulous.

"No, no," I tried to explain. "It wasn't me." I was brought there, I was forced go to along, I was just there, I didn't do anything—but the only word I heard was the *I, I, I,* in every single sentence—

"My God, did anybody get—"

"I got away." There, *I* again. And again, *I* lied to Madeline, *I* lied to the detective, *I* found the lighter. . . .

"Wait." Rhonda knelt before me, caught my hands, waving wildly, and gripped them hard to settle me. "I don't understand. You hid the lighter because you were afraid of getting caught—or you were afraid of getting away with it?"

I stumbled along, as if lip-reading every word. "Both." I shook my head. "I don't know."

"Kerry. It can't be both." She let go of my wrists. I noticed how cold my hands were, and slid them beneath my thighs for warmth. "One way or the other, you have to get this over with."

She reached out to brush a strand of hair from my eyes.

"I know," I sniffed. "But I need you to help me, Rhonda. All year I have. I—"

"Kerry," she said uncomfortably. "This isn't the right time."

"I know, I should have straightened it out before—"

"No, no." She smiled affectionately; at last, something easy. "I mean, right now. See, I'm going out—"

"That's great," I cried, and I pulled my fingers through my

snarled hair. "Because—you know what? I want to get really drunk, that's what I want. I want to—"

"I mean I'm going out with—well, it's a date, Kerry. I've got a date."

"A date," I repeated. "With Brad?"

She shook her head. "No," she said. "Not really."

I took it in slowly. "But what about Brad?"

"He . . . doesn't know, exactly. Look, these are things you'll understand. . . ."

"Rhonda." I panicked at the thought of being alone. "You—I just—I just drove two hundred—"

She took my hands. "Kerry. It's kind of hard to explain—"

I shouted, "I came all this way to see you!"

"You didn't come here to see me," she said, angry now.

"Yes, I—"

"You came to get away from yourself."

I looked around the room, as if I could convince myself I had stumbled into the wrong apartment.

"I'll be back later. Or maybe in the morning. But the couch folds out. And there are sheets in the closet." Rhonda climbed to her feet. "And then we'll spend the whole weekend together, okay? Oh," she said, halfway to the door. "If the phone rings, can you answer it? If it's Brad . . . if it's Brad, tell him I'm at the library, I'll be there late. Tell him you're my cousin—"

"I *am* your cousin."

"Of course. But I mean, tell him you're up for the weekend and I've got a big project, so if he's getting back tonight I can't see him, and—oh, just make something up, okay? You're pretty creative." I didn't smile. She must have noticed. "Tomorrow morning we'll have a big breakfast . . . and I'll make everything clear, okay?"

"Everything," I whispered, "is getting clearer by the minute."

"Okay." She backtracked to the door. "Later."

For the longest time I didn't even move. I thought maybe I could just stay there forever. Right in that chair. Sleep the night all curled up, and nobody would bother me. Maybe Rhonda wouldn't ever come back. Maybe I'd never even have to open the door.

The light in the apartment was growing dim, but I was content to sit there, in the darkness. That was all I wanted. A little peace. It was so quiet—

As quiet as Ms. Trice's basement.

Before they showed up—and why wouldn't they? Kyle knew she never locked her doors. They would have a keg all ready and somebody's boom box, and did I think they would call it off because of me?

That would give them even more pleasure, to think that I was right next door.

I tried to tell myself Ms. Trice would never hear them, and I could sneak back in sometime tomorrow and clean up the beer cans and the overturned furniture and scrub out the stains. That way I wouldn't have to face them. No one would ever know they were there.

I leaned back, shut my eyes, and searched in vain for a comfortable position on Rhonda's old chair.

But even with my eyes closed I kept seeing the darkroom. And the kids, some of them drunk by now, bored, prodding Kevin to entertain them. I saw them playing with the equipment, trying the cameras—

Going through the shelves.

Finding the lighter. Which someone would recognize. Maybe Billy himself, drunk and bitter. They'd all wonder for a while how it ended up there, but it wouldn't take long. Someone would say, *She was going to turn you in, Billy.*

Another voice, after a pause: *Maybe turn us all in.*

Why else would it be here?

Then Linda, after thinking it over. *There was no other reason for her to keep it.*

Would someone defend me? *No, not Kerry, she wouldn't. . . .*

I saw their eyes wander over to Billy, cradling the lighter in his hand.

Why wouldn't she? Think of what she pulled with Kyle.

First their heads, slowly nodding. Then their faces full of spite, and finally, agreement: she was capable of anything.

To hell with her, they'd say. They'd raise a cup to curse my name and turn the music louder. And louder. So loud that someone would hear. If not Ms. Trice, some neighbor—maybe even my mother. And when the police burst in on them, what was to keep them from turning on me in revenge, offering up my name as the one who set the fire?

She was never at the 7-Eleven that night. I lied to protect her. I saw Billy say it, the lighter nestled in his pocket, the urge to confess as distant as his dreams of feeling special at the prom.

But what, I thought, if the police didn't come?

What if no one stumbled on the lighter?

There were still Mr. Trice's bottles of developing fluid, and cleaning alcohol, and the piles of rags. And there were still too many kids, too many beers. Up late, too tired to think straight, and someone always trying to top someone else with the next outrageous stunt.

I saw the flames in Madeline's garage climb up the walls with a will of their own.

I jerked my head as if to shake it clear of worry, and when I knew I couldn't, I leaped to my feet.

Once, when I was little, I used to think that when I turned off the TV all the shows would stop. All the actors, puppets, clowns, even the cartoon figures would stand around the studio waiting, as if no single adventure or story would go on until Kerry Dunbar tuned in again.

Now I knew better.

24

The last twenty miles of the ride back I was slapping my face and sucking in air to ward off sleep.

That was the easy part.

It was way past midnight when I got back. The parking lot at the country club was empty, of course. I raced up the stairs of the portico, still illuminated with floodlights, through the lobby to the ballroom.

Inside, an off-duty waiter leaned against the wall, his jacket over one arm. He looked at me curiously, but I didn't stop. I sure didn't need to ask directions, I had been here half a dozen times with the prom committee—

But the ballroom had never looked like this.

I remembered how intricately we had planned the decorations. How we budgeted for the crepe paper and the spools of shiny ribbon. The nights Paula and I had stayed up, cutting out stars and crescent moons until our fingers ached from squeezing the scissors.

Now, where they once had been suspended from the ceiling, great lengths of crepe paper drooped to the floor. Here and there, underfoot, was a star, a crumpled chrysanthemum. Some of the large cardboard letters which we had wrapped in glistening foil to spell out the school name were missing from their perch.

The tabletops were littered with glasses, coffee cups, plates, an occasional corsage. Bored busboys cleared the debris, and yanked off the rumpled tablecloths. A vacuum cleaner whined along the border of the dance floor.

I stood and stared. I should have been out the door already. I knew they were on their way to Ms. Trice's, and I would have to stop them there.

Then, through the glass doors, I saw someone sitting on the stone wall along the edge of the veranda.

Quickly I passed through the doors and called out, "Excuse me, can you tell me how long ago everyone left?"

A few more steps and I was close enough to see, in the dark, the colors of his tux. An ugly tux. A paisley, swirled . . .

Billy's tux.

You would have thought he'd jerk around in surprise, the way I had rushed up to him. He didn't. He seemed to have all the time in the world.

"I was going to say, 'Hey, I know girls are always late, but not *this* late,'" he said. "But then you'd probably accuse me of being sexist or something, huh?"

"No, Billy." I thought, even with that silly tux, he looked nice.

"Then what did you come for?"

It wasn't the way I imagined he'd be—roaring, dangerous. He was quiet—so far he had hardly turned to face me—and sad. It was a lot worse, this way.

"I came here to find out where they'd gone. Kyle, and Kevin, and the rest."

"Oh." For the first time I heard resentment. "You figure you might as well salvage some of the evening, huh?"

"No." I told him how scared I was about Ms. Trice's house. "Everybody over there—it just made me think of the fire."

"The fire," he said. "That's why you pulled this on me tonight. Right?"

"No—I mean—"

"Do you feel better now? Did I get what I deserved?"

"No, Billy." I straddled the wall to look at him. "I don't feel better." He gazed off, over the golf course beyond the country club. "Billy, the fire was my fault as much as yours. It was just—easier to blame it all on you. I'm sorry."

He rubbed at his eyes.

I leaned in closer. "Billy," I said, just realizing. "You're not drunk."

"Ahh." He seemed embarrassed to admit it. "I guess I didn't feel like it." He allowed himself a little laugh. "Some night, huh? I get stood up for my senior prom, I don't even get drunk—and you know what?" He turned to me. "I still had a good time." He shook his head in wonder. "Without getting drunk. That's kind of scary."

"I'm glad you came. I'm glad you had a good time. I was wrong to put all the blame on you."

"Well, not that wrong." His voice caught, grew soft. "I blame it on me, too. That's what I told Madeline."

I started shivering and couldn't stop. "You told—"

"Yup." He nodded as if he could hardly believe it himself.

"Billy—you never even *talk* to Madeline."

"I did tonight. She was there, and I was there, and—I was feeling good. In spite of you, Kerry." I wanted to shake him for more, but forced myself to wait. "And when I saw her, here, where I never expected to see her—I felt awful again. All at once. Like life would be great if there was a guarantee I'd never have to be reminded of the fire, but Madeline was that reminder, you know?"

"I know."

"And she didn't yell or anything, when I told her. Or try to hit me, or call me those political insults I never even understood. She just—listened. Most people think I'm always joking around. She took me seriously. She didn't even look surprised." He rubbed his face. "I wasn't supposed to tell her. My dad said not to."

"You told your *dad*—"

"Hell, none of us could talk to each other about it, right? So one night with my dad it just came out. I had to tell *somebody*. He said maybe, if they'd agree not to press any charges, he could volunteer his company to build the Abrahams a new garage, and it wouldn't cost them any insurance. He had it all worked out. We'd talk it over with our lawyer, he said, and go to the police on our own terms." He sighed. "He'll be pissed when he finds out I told her."

"Billy," I pressed. "Does Madeline know I was there?"

"Uh-uh," he said. "I didn't mention you. Just me and Kevin. So if the Abrahams say yes—"

I squinted hard, tried to follow his words past "I didn't mention you."

"—we'll start work on it right away. I'm going to help. Great summer job, huh? Full-time, no pay. Wait till Kevin hears he's helping, too."

"But you're sure"—alert now, I phrased it carefully—"she doesn't know about me?"

"Pretty sure," Billy said. He smiled wryly. "I had enough stuff to say about you tonight."

On the drive home I heard the music in my imagination, blasting from Ms. Trice's basement. But after I left the car down the block and stole through the shadows to stand outside her house, I could barely hear it—just enough to know they were really there, and I had to face them. When I crept down the concrete steps and pushed open the door, the reek of beer and smoke poured out at me. I blinked in the dim light. There were plastic cups spread out on top of Ms. Trice's washing machine and dryer. A keg floated on its side in an old washtub, its hose leaking a steady trickle down to the drain in the middle of the floor. Somebody's tuxedo jacket was flung carelessly over the big laundry sink. A hum of voices, occasionally a giggle, came from the other rooms.

Linda stood in the dark hallway, clutching a beer.

"Girl," she said. "You are in some serious trouble."

"I know," I said. And then I couldn't think of anything else except, "You look nice."

"And you," she said, peering closer, "look like shit."

From the darkroom I heard a thunderous belch, and titters of laughter.

"Linda"—I swallowed and said it—"you have to go."

She must not have heard me; instead she was drawing a beer. "Kerry." She turned to me with the cup. "What the hell did you do to Kyle? And to Billy? And what are you even *doing* here?"

"I—" I gazed down at the cup of beer she held out.

"Hey," Linda slurred, "don't get me wrong, I'm glad you're here. We need a little life in this party about now." She put her arm around me and motioned me to the hallway.

"I can't go back there," I said.

"Why not?"

"Why not? You just said, I'm in trouble."

"Aw." She waved her hand. "People get mad, and then they forget. And anyway, what you did didn't affect most of them, right? So you'll hear a few snotty things, and then it's over. It doesn't matter. Come on. What the hell."

We were moving up the hallway now, toward the old darkroom. The music was louder. So were the voices. The smoke was curling in the dim light. Linda still held the beer before me.

Just take it, I thought. Maybe she's right. Gulp it down, and have another. After all, you've got reason to celebrate. The Abrahams will get a new garage, and Billy kept your name out of it. What more could you want? Just get drunk and laugh it off, and sure, some of them will hate you for what you did tonight, but it won't last long.

I remembered what Kyle had said: Linda knows how things work.

"No." I gently pushed the beer away. "Linda. Listen to me. You can't be here."

"What do you mean?" She tried to pause at the edge of the darkroom, but our momentum carried us into the light. I was still looking her way as I sensed the single moment when all the voices died—as if everyone were sucking in a deep breath at once. Then a shrill wind of groans and taunts and incredulous laughter as the voices returned, and several people crowed, "*I don't believe it.*"

Only then did I really look up.

The old red bulb of the darkroom was covered with a bandanna to make it darker still, but I could see all the faces. Greg and his girlfriend, and Heather and Todd, and a couple clutched together in the middle of the room. Kevin Montrose lay on the floor with his head propped up on Mr. Trice's camera bag. He cuddled an empty bottle of tequila as if it were a teddy bear. Heather stepped over him to reclaim a beer. The developing pans were full of cigarette butts. Someone had switched on Mr. Trice's enlarger, and a junior girl whose name I didn't know was trying to make shadow puppets that nobody was able to identify. At last she gave up and began to flash the light in people's eyes, cackling maniacally.

I reached out to the boom box, ejected the tape, and said it quickly. "You all have to go."

"Kerry," Linda warned. "Don't—"

"You have to go. This wasn't my idea."

"Honey," Heather hissed, "didn't anyone tell you you're not in charge of the prom anymore?"

On the floor, Kevin stirred. "What's she saying?"

Then everyone at once in a blare of abuse: outright curses and quiet snide comments, insults flung in my face, laughter at the very thought that they might leave. Greg Del Sandro climbed to his feet.

"What makes you think you can ask everyone over here—"

"I never did. That was Kyle."

"Well, you sure as hell coulda said something before now."

"You're right," I said. "I'm sorry. I should have."

"She likes to wait for the last minute," Heather sneered. "Ask Kyle."

Then bitter giggling ran around the room. I tried to follow it to its source, but I only saw dead eyes in grinning faces. My own eyes stung with smoke. "You still have to go."

Greg crossed his arms. "How you gonna get rid of us?"

I looked to Linda for help, but she was straddling the arm of the threadbare old sofa, watching me coolly.

"You gonna call the police?" Greg raised an eyebrow.

"If I have to," I said.

Someone snorted at that. Someone else laughed.

"Bitch." That was Heather. I brushed it off, and stepped aside to clear the doorway. "Just leave," I said again. I nudged Kevin with my foot. "Wake up. Take the keg. I'm not cleaning up after you." I knew I would, though. I would do anything to be rid of them. And a few were already moving to the door. I looked to Linda, but she only threw up her hands and sighed as if she weren't responsible for any of this.

"Okay," Greg said with a touch of surrender in his voice. I slumped with relief. "*Okay.*" But he was talking way too loud, purposely loud, as if he wanted to wake Ms. Trice—or someone else. "Okay, well, somebody better tell Kyle."

Linda elbowed him. "Greg, shut up."

"No, really, tell Kyle. We can't leave him here—"

"Where is he?" I demanded. Kevin Montrose's belly rumbled with amusement.

"Greg, you are such a jerk," Linda said.

"He's in back," Greg said with a leer. "You better go tell him yourself." Then laughter again, the metal grating of the keg hauled up the stairs, and their voices slowly faded into the night. By now I had inched my way down the darkened hallway, groping along the wall for where the corridor opened into the last, large room.

"Kyle?" I called.

I felt eyes on my back, and caught Kevin lingering by the basement door, grinning stupidly, until he wobbled his way up after the others.

"Kyle?" I eased in until I was beyond the pool of light, in full darkness. "Are you here?"

In the shadows to my left I sensed movement, and I almost jumped. Then it was clear: breathing. Then giggling. The type of giggling you didn't do alone.

His voice, cocky as ever: "Couldn't keep away from me, huh?"

I knew somewhere overhead there was a fixture and a bare bulb. I swung my arms until I found the dangling string.

They yelped at the light and my own eyes flinched shut, but not before I saw them.

Kyle was lounging in an overstuffed easy chair, his long legs stretched out, his tuxedo shirt half open. Even in that instant I saw the killer smile. And huddled on his lap, the girl, kissing him in a smothering embrace.

The girl was Jessica.

She recovered well. By the time I forced my eyes open she was standing, tugging up her lace stockings before smoothing her hands down her tight, sleek dress. Only then did she turn to face me, and in the harsh overhead light the smudge of mascara left exaggerated shadows under her eyes.

She only said two things to me. The first was terse, and vulgar, and unlike anything I had ever heard her say.

The second was after she had stepped into her high heels and was almost past me, pausing just to share an insolent glance. "You are such a *loser*, Kerry."

When she was down the hallway I turned to Kyle and said, "You, too. You have to go."

He took his time buttoning his shirt and shrugging into his

jacket. I knew it was all for my benefit. He cocked his head to one side and nodded to where Jessica had gone. "It could have been you, you know."

"No," I said to him. "It couldn't."

He laughed cynically.

"*Listen to me.*" I grabbed the front of his shirt. "It couldn't be me. As hard as I tried. I know that now." His eyes tried to flit away from me, but I wouldn't let them. I grabbed his jaw and held his face so he had to meet my eyes. And then I watched his face let go, like a hand releasing its grip. There was something sad about him now, something—vulnerable. It was the kind of look a person could fall in love with. I wished I'd seen it more.

My hand slipped to his collar, and I straightened his bow tie. "You'd better go," I whispered. "Everyone's waiting for you."

I waited, and when I was sure they weren't coming back, I started to clean. I did everything in slow motion, even dropped the shards of broken glass one by one into a bag to minimize the noise. I turned on the tap just enough to get a trickle to wet the rags I used to wipe the sticky concrete floor. As far as I could tell, nothing had been damaged, and my memory helped me replace Mr. Trice's lens cases and equipment into the same spots they had rested for years.

How long Ms. Trice had been watching me, I didn't know. When I first spotted her I leaped with shock—she looked like a ghost in her nightgown, there by the basement stairs.

I couldn't speak, for shame.

She nodded as she glanced around. Her nostrils twitched in the still smoky air. "I've been to a few of these," she said.

I looked up at her from where I knelt in the hallway, scrubbing. "Ms. Trice," I mumbled. "It's—it's not the way it seems."

With some difficulty she took the rag from my hands,

wrung it out in the sink, wet it again, and crouched down beside me.

"It never is." She smiled, and started in on a sticky blotch of beer. "Care to tell me about it?"

I did, too; we had the rest of the night to talk. She told me some episodes of her own that she wasn't so proud of, and they weren't quite the same as mine, of course, but I was beginning to realize no one else's ever could be. "Did you put those stories in your book?" I asked. "Or were you . . . ashamed?"

She laughed. "Of course I was ashamed. But I put them in. They were important, after all."

"You know what?" I said. "I think I've been away from your book too long."

It was after dawn now, and we could see the gray light through the basement windows.

"Kerry, you should get some sleep. Why don't you just curl up in the darkroom? You were always so cozy there." She chuckled. "And it's probably never been so tidy."

"I'd like to," I said, and yawned. The quiet of the little room was tempting. "But I have something I have to take care of."

"At this hour?"

"Uh-huh. It's late enough already."

My legs were cramped from hours of kneeling. I wavered as I stood upright and massaged them, and then I stepped back into the darkroom, groped toward the back of the shelf until I found the lighter and gripped it tightly.

"Is it something I can help you with?" she asked from the hallway.

I came out of the darkroom and shook my head. "Thanks, Ms. Trice." I glanced around the basement. "I think it's time I started cleaning up my messes on my own."

25

I huddled in the shelter of a tree at the edge of Madeline's yard and made my calculations.

I didn't mention you.

Billy's words kept looping through my head as I stared at her house, searching for signs that she was awake.

I could still get out of here. Let her wonder all she might whether I was there the night of the fire, she'd never know for sure. I just wouldn't have to see her, that's all. And if we ran into each other, in the summer, I could just make some small talk, and smile. I was good at that, that certain type of smile that said nothing, and pleased everyone.

I must have dozed off, waiting, for when a gray sedan pulled to the curb in front and parked awkwardly, I awoke with a start and knew I was stuck there. A minute later, Madeline climbed out and the sedan drove off. She wore a flouncy gown—black, of course—with a modest neckline, and her hair radiated grandly over her shoulders as she trudged up the walk, barefoot, her heels in her hand.

"Hey!" I heard myself call out. "Hey, Prom Queen."

She stopped at my voice and squinted until she spotted me in the dim light.

"Hi," I said.

"Hi." She came to me through the wet grass as nonchalantly as if she were wearing one of her loose skirts and sandals.

So much for the easy part. We stood a few feet apart, as stiff as actors in the school play, and ran our eyes up and down each other until somebody had to speak.

"So"—I stood up tall, but all that came out was—"how was the prom?"

How was the prom? Coward! I cursed myself. Get on with it! But Madeline threw her head back and rolled her eyes upward, and though the prom was the last thing I wanted to hear about, I welcomed the diversion. "The music was awful. The food was terrible. The kids were obnoxious. Ken Doll had to dance with every single girl there, including me. My feet were screaming in these heels. Andrew's allergies were killing him and he sniffled all over me. The dance floor was like a crowded elevator. The maître d' was part reptile. The teachers all sat at their table and stared at us as if we were convicts. . . ."

She drew a breath.

"I loved it," she added. "Don't you dare tell anyone."

"You don't have to worry about that," I said. "I don't have any friends left to tell." I knew we could keep this up about the prom for quite a while, no matter how thin our laughter sounded. Just the thought of that helped me go on. "Mad. You talked to Billy Stockton, didn't you?"

She turned instinctively, and then stared straight ahead. "I always knew he was there that night," she said. We had drifted to the far edge of her yard, beyond the spot where the garage had stood, down to where the lawn sloped to the stream. On a low, flat rock overlooking the water we settled ourselves. "And Kevin Montrose. One of them, certainly. There were . . . those words. *Jew bitch.* That drawing. My *portrait.*" She tried a bitter grin, but even that was painful.

"That's what made me certain, the drawing. It made me realize I'd been seeing Kevin's artwork scratched into desks for years. He's got a really recognizable style, too, if you like stick figures." She flung her shoes aside. "The police said that wasn't enough to make any arrests, they could only ask questions, and everybody had alibis." She sighed. "But I just knew, all along, it was Kevin. And Billy."

"And me," I said. She didn't move. "Did you hear me? I was there."

She drew her knees up under her chin, and clasped her arms around them.

"Mad, I—"

"Stop it."

"You knew," I said, piecing it together, and then I shouted, as if I were the one hurling accusations, "didn't you? You always knew!"

"Stop it, I don't want to—"

"Look," I said, digging into the pocket of my jeans. I held the lighter out to her in my open palm.

"What's"—I saw her dim recognition, from a long-ago party—"what's that supposed to—"

"This is what started the fire."

"Well, see?" she said. "That's *Billy's*."

"But why do you think I have it? I was there. *I was part of it*."

She laid her face against her knees, away from me.

I whispered, "Why didn't you ever ask me . . . if I was there?"

"I tried. I tried lots of times, and I always backed down. I told myself, Kerry's a friend."

"Some friend," I muttered.

"I'd say, Of course she wasn't there, and that was easier than confronting you. And sometimes . . . I'd even believe it." She scrunched up her shoulders. "There are all sorts of ways to lie to yourself."

"You're right," I said. "I've probably tried them all."

She motioned to the lighter with her chin. "Why'd you keep it? To protect Billy?"

"At first. And later, to protect myself *from* Billy. But more than all of that, keeping it made me sure I'd remember."

Mad lifted her head. "You didn't think you'd *remember*?"

"Of course I would. But I wanted more than just *remembering*. That was what frightened me." My voice took off on its own now, shrill and panicky. "That I'd just *remember,* but I wouldn't *feel* anything. I wouldn't feel *guilty,* I wouldn't feel *responsible,* I'd be one of those people who learns to shrug and toss things off and say, Well, what's done is done. . . ."

"Give it to me," Madeline said. I laid the lighter in her hand. For a few seconds she stared at the girl in the bikini— and then she flung the lighter into the center of the stream. With a tiny splash, it disappeared.

"How do you feel?" she asked.

"What do you mean?" I cried. "I feel *horrible.*"

She gestured to where the last few ripples were swept up by the current. "So what'd you need that for?"

We sat silently, huddled against the morning chill.

"Well," Madeline said, "Billy made this proposal. I don't know what my parents will do. Something about his father's construction company, rebuilding the garage. And him, helping. Even Kevin."

"I want to be there, too," I said.

"You?" I saw her smile, and knew exactly why: she was picturing me in construction clothes, hammer and tape measure dangling from my tool belt, staggering under a load of lumber.

"What's the matter?" I sat up, as if my pride had been damaged. "Are you saying construction's just a *man's job*?"

She did the best thing she could have done; she reached over and put her arm around me. I hugged her back. But as she started to speak, I pulled back abruptly and stared. I felt my mouth drop open.

"What's the matter?" she asked, alarmed.

"You're wearing makeup, aren't you?"

"Auggh." She grimaced, and hid her head in her hands. "No guilt trips about rabbits, okay?"

I hugged her. "Okay."

"Kerry. Just what did you pull, last night, with Billy Stockton? Everybody was talking about you."

"I thought I was doing it for you, Mad."

"For me?"

"I wanted to get back at him, I guess. For the fire. And for the stuff Kevin scrawled on the wall while Billy just sat there. And all the parties, and those jokes he'd tell, where people just stood around and laughed, Linda and Heather and Greg. And sometimes, me."

"You *laughed*?"

"Sometimes," I confessed. "I was afraid not to." I took her hand. "I'm not afraid anymore," I said.

"Well." Madeline exhaled mightily, like a diver reaching the surface. "I wasn't afraid to tell him what I thought. Really shook him up, too. Here he just tells me how sorry he is about the garage, and I hardly blink. He thinks he's getting off easy—and then I let him have it, about those jokes. I made him tell me one. Then another. And then I made him explain them. Why they were supposed to be funny. He couldn't, of course. He just squirmed and looked miserable. So you know what I said? 'Congratulations, Billy. You've just spent the last ten minutes talking to a real Jew. Now the next time you tell one of your jokes—' 'I won't,' he promised. 'The next time you tell one, at least you'll know how stupid it is.' He said he was sorry, he really was. He couldn't understand why I could stay so calm about the garage and get so upset about the jokes. He said, 'I never thought I was doing any harm.' 'Billy,' I told him, 'a *garage* you can rebuild.'"

We watched the sunlight glimmer on the surface of the stream.

"At least," she said, yawning, "he learned *something* in high school."

From the water a lone bullfrog croaked his single note, over and over. With each deep *thunk* we began to laugh more. Soon we were snickering uncontrollably.

"You can tell it's a male," I said as the croaking continued. "It's so loud and obnoxious."

"Let's find him," Mad said suddenly. She waded down into the stream, the hem of her dress floating up around her knees. "I've had it with males. Any species, they're all the same."

"You're crazy," I said, laughing. "What about your dress?"

She took a couple more steps. "Just *when,*" she asked, "am I going to wear something like *this* again?"

In a few seconds I was there beside her, and we coiled, motionless, until the bullfrog resumed his call, and then we splashed after him like lunatics. The water was cold and we rooted through the muck until we sprung the poor frog from his cover. Once I even had my hands on him, though he was so slick and strong he wriggled free the very moment I howled in triumph. For a while longer we searched, and then we just gave up and started splashing each other until we were completely drenched.

After a while Madeline wanted to change.

"Spoilsport," I moaned as she climbed up the bank toward her house.

"Kerry, you want to stay like this, soaked through?"

"Maybe I do," I said, trudging beside her. "I don't know when I've felt better."

26

It never rained on graduation, Ken Doll said. The board of education wouldn't allow it. He said it every graduation, too, except the years when it rained. The audience chuckled politely and he went booming on about *crossroads* and *decisions* and *unforgettable memories* and *how proud he was of each and every single young person up here today*—all the things I had never realized that graduates didn't think about. Instead we thought, God, it's hot in this gown or Please don't let me trip when they call my name.

Row after row of parents, friends, underclassmen, relatives, a few of the town police on overtime, alumni, and strangers stared curiously up at us where we sat in rickety folding chairs flanking the Senior Steps. We might have been a special attraction at the zoo. Once I had spotted my parents (some genius on the seating committee had placed them next to each other, and I had to laugh to see how stiffly they sat so their elbows wouldn't touch) there wasn't much else to do but actually listen to the speeches. I didn't get any awards; I certainly wasn't valedictorian. Kyle did well. Ken Doll must have called his name four times for various honors. Each time Kyle came up to receive an award, Jessica scurried up the center aisle with a camera. Just before Kyle turned to go back to his seat he paused, momentarily, to give her a good angle for the photo. His pose was so brief it was almost imperceptible, but I knew better.

Then, afterward, in the big grassy circle in front of the school, there was a mob of people to wedge through. I bumped shoulders and stepped on feet—it was as jammed as a department store the day before Christmas—and when I saw my mother I hugged her, and I wiped the tears from her cheeks so she wouldn't get embarrassed. My dad stood awkwardly nearby. Thank God he had his camera to occupy him. It was a new one: big and complicated, and he still wasn't sure how to use it.

Just as he was positioning me for a photo, Mr. Hyams strolled over.

"Kerry Dunbar." He held me at arm's length, looked at me with those watery blue eyes, and said, "I still say you should be going to college."

"I am going to college."

"But you should be going while you're young," he continued.

"Mr. Hyams, I'll still be young next fall. I'm just going to work for a year, and—"

"And flip hamburgers in some fast-food place," Mr. Hyams scoffed. "Or waitress. Or be somebody's secretary."

"No, I won't be doing that." I was going to be working with my mother. The county supervisor had found enough funding to set up a compromised version of her original proposal: a halfway house for girls who wanted to keep their babies but couldn't live at home; counseling for abortion referrals; and presentations on birth control and AIDS prevention for adolescent youth groups. ("That'll be fun," Teddy teased. "You'll get to show how condoms fit over cucumbers. You'll never eat vegetables again.") When I asked my mother how the supervisor was able to find the money, she said she didn't know, but she suspected it had something to do with a crazy, obsessed woman who started nagging him day after day. And when I asked, "What woman was that?" she broke into a big smile. Duh, Kerry.

At first, because my mother got me the job, I was worried about charges of nepotism, but the pay was so low and the work was so hard you probably had to hire your own kid—no one else would do it.

I tried again. "Instead of going to school right away, I'll be—"

"Well, if you ask me"—Mr. Hyams turned to my dad— "she's A-1 college material."

That was when my dad said, "Well, it's really my fault she's not going this fall."

"Beg pardon?" Mr. Hyams asked.

"It's my fault. The way I run my—well, my—"

"Uh, Dad . . ."

"Okay. My finances. That's true, Kerry, isn't it?"

"Okay," I said, as if I were a gymnastics judge awarding points.

"You thought I was going to say, the way I run my life, right?"

"*Dad.*"

"Sorry, but I've just got to be—"

"Honest," I groaned.

"Exactly. And I haven't been very responsible. Kerry's too polite to tell you that, Mister—what was it again?"

"Hyams," he croaked. I could see he had never expected to be in a conversation like this and was dying for a way out.

"But it's true, isn't it, hon?"

"No. Well . . . sure. But"—I turned to Mr. Hyams—"it's also because I'm not sure Ridley's right for me. I'm not sure what's right for me, yet."

Mr. Hyams smiled feebly.

"So," I said, "I don't mind taking a year or so to figure that out."

"Hey," my dad rescued us all, "let's get a photo." He motioned the two of us together. Mr. Hyams put his arm around me, and as I glanced over I saw his usual grin returning comfortably to his face, and his hand rose with two fingers aloft in the peace sign.

"Hold it," my dad said, peering through his camera. Just before he snapped the shutter release, I raised my hand in the peace sign, too.

Then for a while I moved through the crowd on my own, saying "Good-bye" and "Keep in touch." There were a few to whom I really meant it, too. One was Billy, and I hugged him, hard. The Abrahams had agreed to his father's offer, but they insisted that Billy and Kevin do community service as well. Billy was helping out at their temple day-care center after school.

"How's it going?" I asked him.

"Okay. It's fun, really. Except"—he grimaced—"I get a little sore playing horsey three hours a day."

I was ready to find my parents again before my father had to leave, when Teddy and I bumped into each other. He did an exaggerated double take, his mortarboard falling off.

"You behaved yourself tonight," I said. We laughed and he circled me with his arms and pulled me close. He only had to take a step or two and hum a waltz tune to get us both giggling. I didn't let go of him right away.

"Teddy," I said. "Let's get together this summer."

"I *can't*," he moaned. "I'll be in Washington. You know, blazing trails? My internship?"

"That's right," I remembered.

"*Now* you ask me."

"I guess I have a knack for the last minute." I smiled.

"Well, there's tomorrow. We can go to the beach."

"I can't," I said. For tomorrow I was starting my other

summer job; tomorrow we started on the Abrahams' new garage. "I'd love to." I pulled his graduation gown to me and laid my brow against his. "I mean it, I'd really love to, but I have . . . a commitment. I promised."

"Well," he said with a smile, "a promise is a promise."

"I know," I said. He kissed me and I let him go, and after he gave me one last wave I turned, and stood at the edge of the circle. It was getting dark now. Already the high school was only a large, distant silhouette. The fireflies were out, and the white gowns of the girls glowed faintly in the soft glimmer of the streetlights. Voices hushed and trailed off. A laugh rang out for a second, and soon the nervous rhythm of the crickets was everywhere. Faces were hard to identify; you couldn't tell who someone was until you were right up close. I watched couples, and families, and clusters of friends, and here and there a person alone, drift to the edge of the circle and into the shadows, where I lost them in the darkness. I knew it was my time, too, to go, but I had promised Madeline I would see her again before I left. It was harder now—I almost had to grope my way in the waning light—but I didn't mind. I was confident I'd find her.